GODS AND WARRIORS

WARRIOR BRONZE

MICHELLE PAVER

Book 5

Dial Books for Young Readers

Dial Books for Young Readers
Penguin Young Readers Group
An imprint of Penguin Random House LLC
375 Hudson Street
New York, NY 10014

First published in Great Britain 2016 by Puffin Books Ltd
Published in the United States 2017 by Dial Books for Young Readers

Maps and illustrations by Fred Van Deelen

Logo design by James Fraser

Printed in the U.S.A.

ISBN 9780803738843

1 3 5 7 9 10 8 6 4 2

Design by Nancy R. Leo-Kelly
Text set in ITC Galliard Std

THE WORLD OF GODS AND WARRIORS

MAP of AKEA

ARKADIA

AKEA

Mycenae

The
Ancestor
Peak

Mount
Lykas

MESSENIA

Dentra

Lapithos
plains

Marshes

Main Pass

LYKONIA

Crows
Lookout
Post

Eastern
Mountains

N
W   E
S

I

Hylas hauled on the oars and the coast of Messenia loomed closer. They'd set off under cover of darkness, but the wind had torn away the clouds, and now the Moon was shining as bright as day.

Glancing over his shoulder, he saw Pirra's pale, tense face—and behind her, the rocky headland they had to reach. To the left lay a misty sweep of marshes; to the right, dark towering cliffs. On top of these, he made out the red fires of a lookout post and the black forms of Crow warriors cutting across the flames. His spine prickled. He could almost feel their arrows between his shoulder blades.

Every splash of the oars, every slap of waves against the boat, sent his heart racing. Sound travels farther at night, especially over water. Surely the Crows would hear?

Even if they didn't, it was only a matter of time before they spotted the little rowing boat. It must stand out like a black leaf on a silver Sea: a black leaf in which crouched a boy, a girl with a falcon dozing on her shoulder, and a very seasick lion.

Havoc sat in front of him, miserably panting. Ropes of spit hung from her jaws, and her flanks were heaving. Earlier, she'd vomited all over him. His tunic stank, and behind him, Pirra was breathing through her mouth.

Now the lioness was gazing with longing at the cool black water. Hylas prayed that she wouldn't decide to leap in for a swim; the warriors on the cliff wouldn't fail to hear that.

Havoc lurched to her feet, rocking the boat so violently that it nearly capsized.

"Havoc, keep *still*!" hissed Pirra.

"Get down!" whispered Hylas, desperately trying to restrain the lioness while gripping both oars in one hand. But Havoc was twice his size and many times stronger; she easily shook him off.

The commotion woke Echo, who flew skyward with loud indignant squawks.

"That's all we need!" breathed Pirra.

Hylas gave up on Havoc and grimly applied himself to the oars.

To his relief, she seemed to have forgotten about her swim: She was pricking her ears, eagerly snuffing the air. They were nearing the headland at last.

At its tip, Hylas spotted an overhang; maybe they could hide the boat underneath. As he maneuvered closer, he saw Pirra take a scrap of gold from her pouch and drop it over the side, her lips moving in a silent prayer to her Goddess. He guessed what it was: *Help us find Issi, and the dagger of*

Koronos . . . Help us vanquish the Crows . . . In his head, he said his own prayer to the Lady of the Wild Things. He tried to take comfort from the *wedjat* amulet on his chest.

A distant splash out to Sea—and for a moment, he forgot about the Crows and eagerly scanned the waves. Dolphins had been in his thoughts since they'd reached these waters, but so far he'd spotted none. And now, no silver back arched out of the waves, and he caught no *pfft!* of dolphin breath.

The prow bumped against rock, and Havoc leaped soundlessly onto the headland, twitching her tail and panting with relief. Pirra went next with the rope, then Hylas. Together they wedged the boat beneath the overhang, hating the echoing scrape of wood against stone. As Hylas bent to secure the boat, he glimpsed a small black sea cave farther in; that must be why the echoes were so loud.

"Looks like there's a path up this ridge," murmured Pirra.

He didn't reply. That smell on the wind . . . The tarry, eye-watering stink of mastic bushes. He hadn't smelled that in two years. Two long years on the run, and at last he was back.

He had the strangest sense that everything that had happened to him since: being a slave in the mines of Thalakrea, seeking Pirra on Keftiu, finding and losing the dagger in Egypt—that none of it had been real. He felt as if he were twelve years old again, on that terrible night when the Crows had attacked his camp and killed his dog Scram, and his sister Issi had gone missing . . .

Pirra touched his shoulder and he jumped. "Hylas, are you all right? Are you having a vision?"

"No, I . . ."

"Then come on, or we'll be spotted!"

Rocks were rough beneath his bare feet. Thorns scratched his shins. No sound came from the warriors on the cliff.

To his left, a thin mist hid the marshes. He had no idea how far they stretched inland, or how to get past them, or where to go after that. He'd grown up in Lykonia, on the other side of the mountains; he knew nothing of Messenia. Except that it was vast and ruled by the Crows; and that somewhere in its vastness, his sister might be hiding—if she was still alive.

He and Pirra had paid the ship's captain well to bring them to Messenia, but as the coast had risen into view, the captain had refused to take them any farther.

"Too dangerous," he'd growled. "There's fierce fighting between the Crows and the rebels, both here and in Lykonia." Instead, he'd steered as close to the cliffs as he dared, then he gave them the rowing boat and wished them luck. "Though I don't give much for your chances, the Crows are everywhere. Don't look to the peasants for help; they're too frightened, they'd only turn you in. And whatever you do, *stay out of the marshes*, not even the Crows go in there. The Marsh Dwellers used to be friendly, but since the Crows came, they've changed, they'll kill anyone who ventures in . . ."

The captain had also told them that a dolphin had been seen in these waters. "Swimming back and forth along the coast," he'd said in awe, "as if it's—*waiting* for someone." Hylas' thoughts had flown to Spirit, the dolphin they'd befriended two summers before. He'd kept watch from the ship, leaning overboard, whistling softly for his friend, and several curious dolphins had swum closer—but not the big one with the scars on his nose.

The hot, tarry night wind brought him back to the headland. Forget about Spirit, he told himself. What could Spirit do against the Crows?

But he still longed for the dolphin to appear.

He and Pirra hadn't climbed far when it occurred to him that Havoc hadn't yet passed them. She should have; she was hungry and she must be eager to hunt.

He glanced back—and his stomach turned over. *"Havoc!"* he whispered urgently. *"Come here!"*

"Havoc, no!" breathed Pirra, beside him.

The lioness ignored them. She was still on the tip of the headland, gazing at the water that rocked so temptingly within reach.

The lure proved too strong. As Hylas started down to her, Havoc leaped in with an enormous splash. It was far louder than any fish could make. If that didn't bring the warriors, nothing would.

The night wind hissed through the thornscrub. Waves slapped the rocks. No shouts came from above.

Havoc surfaced sleekly, slitting her eyes with pleasure:

She was cool again, and *clean!* Once back on the rocks, she shook herself noisily, then bounded past Hylas and Pirra and vanished into the scrub.

Still no sounds from the cliffs. With pounding hearts, Hylas and Pirra resumed their climb, hoping to find some way along the left flank of the headland, then past the marshes . . .

Echo swept over their heads and lit onto a boulder right in front of Pirra. The falcon was agitated, half spreading her wings and glaring with gaping beak. She flew off again, uttering shrill *eck-eck-ecks.*

"What is it?" whispered Hylas. "What's she seen?"

Pirra stood tensely, peering at the top of the headland. "Someone's coming!"

"I heard a splash!" shouted a man's voice, muffled through the rocks.

"We're on the *coast,* you idiot," sneered a second man. "Things splash. Waves. Fish."

"This was much bigger than a fish."

Hylas and Pirra swam deeper into the sea cave at the back of the overhang. They'd reached it in a headlong scramble, but once they'd slipped inside, it occurred to Hylas that it might turn into a trap, not a hiding place.

The cave was deep, and too narrow for him and Pirra to swim abreast. He led the way, easing past slimy rocks and prickly sea urchins.

The water grew abruptly colder: He guessed that the

Sun never reached this far in. They came to a dead end and huddled together, rocking in the swell and breathing the stink of rotting seaweed. It was shallow enough to stand, but the roof was so low, there was only just space to keep their heads above water.

Hylas strained for the sound of feet coming closer, but all he heard was the echoing slap of the Sea. In the gloom, Pirra's eyes were wide and dark. Her long hair clung in black snakes to her throat, and her lips looked black too.

Ahead of them, the cave mouth was a disc of moonlit Sea so small that he could blot it out with his fist; the cave was deeper than he'd thought. He glimpsed the prow of the rowing boat. He prayed it wouldn't drift loose and betray them to the Crows.

Cold was seeping into his bones; he had to clench his teeth to stop them chattering. Beside him, he felt Pirra shivering uncontrollably.

Suddenly, she stiffened and clutched his arm. "Did you hear that?" she mouthed. "They're climbing down toward us!"

He heard it too: the clatter of pebbles and scrape of feet as Crow warriors made their way down the headland.

At that moment, something soft and slimy brushed against his flank. Stifling a cry, he tried to push it off, but now it was slithering up his chest. It was smooth and boneless, yet alarmingly strong. He thought of giant eels with teeth that never let go, not even if you cut off their heads. He drew his knife—but Pirra grabbed his wrist and shook her head urgently.

"Octopus," she hissed in his ear.

Hylas struggled to keep still while the creature's snakelike limbs gripped and sucked their way up his chest and onto his shoulder. He turned his head, and two bulging black eyes stared into his. The octopus seemed to realize that he wasn't a rock, turned pale with fright, and plopped back into the water.

Pebbles rattled, and the scrape of feet came closer. It sounded as if the warriors were climbing all the way to the point.

Pirra gave a twitch and a muffled yelp. "Something stung me!" she whispered.

Hylas felt a burning pain on his calf, then another on his thigh. Desperately, he jabbed underwater with his knife. Pirra was doing the same, her lips peeled back in a grimace.

Pain seared his palm, and a squelchy mass shot through his fingers, leaving them on fire. *Jellyfish*, he thought.

"Jellyfish!" breathed Pirra.

At the mouth of the cave, more pebbles fell with a splash.

"Did you hear that?" cried a man's voice, shockingly loud. By the sound of it, he was at the edge of the overhang. If he knelt and peered underneath . . .

"So what?" jeered the other man. "Whatever it is, it's a long way out!"

Pirra was curled into a ball, frantically trying to fend off the jellyfish without making any noise. Hylas tried to shield her with his body, while scraping away the creatures with his knife. In his mind, he saw the Crow warriors crouching above them. He saw their black rawhide armor and the cruel glint of bronze spears. He could almost smell their oniony sweat and the bitter reek of the ash they smeared on their skin . . .

This time, he too heard the splash, far out to Sea.

"There!" cried the first warrior. "*Now* d'you hear it?"

"Who cares about that?" snarled the second one. "I heard something closer . . ."

More pebbles rained down from the overhang.

"Something's down there," said the second man. "And it isn't a fish."

The splash came again. This time, both warriors gasped. "What *is* that?" cried the second one.

Hylas heard Pirra breathe in with a hiss. She was staring at the disc of moonlit Sea beyond the cave mouth. Then he saw it too: a dolphin arching out of the Sea, spouting glittering jets of light as it raced toward them down the path of the Moon.

Nearer and nearer it sped. With a catch at his heart, Hylas saw its sleek silver back and the scars on its nose. He watched it swerve in front of them and make a great shining leap, crashing down and sending a large wave drenching the headland where the warriors were standing.

For a heartbeat, as Spirit arched once more out of the water, his large dark eye met Hylas.' *Thank you, my friend,* Hylas told him silently. Then the dolphin was gone.

The water rocked. Spirit did not reappear.

Seawater was raining from the rim of the overhang, and the warriors were spluttering. "*That's* what you heard," growled the first one. "A dolphin! Let's get out of here!"

"How was I s'pposed to know?" snapped the sneering

one, who was sneering no longer. "Anyway, it better not come back!"

Sounds of a scuffle. "Put that spear down! Don't you know dolphins are *sacred*?"

"All right, all right! Let's go. We're too close to the marshes, and those Dwellers come and go like ghosts . . ." Their voices faded as they trudged up the slope.

"Thank you, Spirit," murmured Pirra.

Hylas didn't reply. He longed for the dolphin to come again; but something told him that Spirit was already far away, swimming out to Sea to rejoin his pod.

The jellyfish had gone as swiftly as they'd come, leaving stinging blisters on Hylas' shoulders and chest. Pirra was wincing and rubbing her arms. "Somehow I don't want to climb that headland anymore," she muttered.

"Nor me. We'll have to get back in the boat and take our chances up the coast."

Which way? East of the headland, the coast was directly overlooked by the Crows. "But if we go west," said Pirra, "how do we avoid the marshes?"

"The captain said there's a stream between them and the headland. If we can find it, we can follow it inland—"

"If," she said.

After the chill of the cave, it was a relief to get out into the hot autumn night. The moonlight was so bright, it made them blink, but a bank of white mist had crept in, and hid the coast from view.

When they'd dragged the boat from beneath the overhang, Pirra took the oars and Hylas stayed in the water, swimming with one hand on the prow. To find the stream, he was going to try a trick he'd learned from Periphas, the ex-slave who'd been his friend after they'd escaped Thalakrea.

"Fresh water feels colder than the Sea," he explained to Pirra. "With luck, I can find the stream by feel."

He was also hoping against hope that Spirit might return. But as they started off, with Pirra quietly rowing and he swimming one-handed, guiding them as close to the rocks as he dared, he saw no gleaming gray back and felt no smooth dolphin snout lightly caressing his flank. Only a shoal of small silvery fishes kept him company, swarming and flickering around his legs. Spirit wouldn't come again. He could feel it.

He began to lose heart. What are we *doing* here? he thought bitterly. The Crows have the dagger. We don't even know where it is. And for all I know, Issi might be long dead.

In the two years she'd been missing, he'd tried not to think of her, it hurt too much. But now that he was back, it was harder to keep the memories at bay. She kept butting into his thoughts: his noisy, argumentative, infuriating little sister . . .

In the boat, Pirra gave a convulsive shudder. "Something's wrong," she hissed.

Now Hylas felt it too. It wasn't the stabbing headaches, the sickness, and flashing lights that he got before a vision; it was dread, pressing on his heart like a hand.

Echo lit onto Pirra's shoulder, and she put up one hand and touched the falcon's foot. Echo sat hunched, with her head sunk in her shoulders. Pirra frowned.

"What's wrong with her?" breathed Hylas.

"I don't know," she whispered. "It feels as if—as if she's *scared*."

"*Echo*? She's not scared of anything! Except ants."

"I know. But I feel it too."

Suddenly, the fish around Hylas fled in a silent silver explosion, and for an instant, something cut across the Moon. It was moving too fast for him to see if it was bird or cloud, but it was huge, and as the light briefly died, dread rushed through him like a dark wind.

The thing in the Sky was gone as swiftly as it had come, and once again, the Moon shone bright. Neither Hylas nor Pirra spoke. They didn't want to voice their suspicions out loud, but both were thinking of the Angry Ones: the terrible spirits of air and darkness who were worshipped by the Crows.

As they moved forward, Hylas felt the water turn abruptly colder. "I think we've found that stream," he murmured.

"It *can't* be!" whispered Pirra. "These are the marshes!"

Through shifting veils of fog, the stream showed as a strip of dull silver, flanked by man-high reeds with dry brown heads that exhaled a swampy breath of decay. Here and there, a low hunched willow appeared in the mist, or a tall poplar, standing guard. One of the poplars had died and fallen across the mouth of the stream. In its white skeletal branches, three black cormorants roosted with their heads beneath their wings.

"We can't go in there," said Pirra. Even the throbbing ring of night crickets and the low *eep-eep* of frogs sounded a warning.

Ahead of them, the reeds stirred—and Havoc appeared, with a large fish wriggling in her jaws. The lioness cast a casual glance at Hylas and Pirra, then leaped onto the dead tree trunk—waking the cormorants, who flew off into the mist—and sprawled full length, with her hind legs dangling on either side of the trunk. With the fish grasped firmly between her forepaws, she started noisily crunching it up.

Hylas breathed out. "She doesn't seem too worried."

"Of course not," snapped Pirra, "she's a *lion*!"

Hauling himself into the boat, he wrung out his long fair hair. "Well, I think we'll have to risk it. After all, the captain said the Marsh Dwellers are Outsiders, like me—"

"And how will you get a chance to tell them who you are?" demanded Pirra. "The captain also said they shoot on sight!"

"Pirra, we can't go back, and for all we know, these marshes stretch right along the coast! Have you got a better idea?"

They'd left the boat tied to the skeleton tree, but they were finding it hard to follow the stream, as the reeds didn't want to let them through. They were dense and tussocky, except where they opened without warning onto treacherous, sucking pools of mud.

Havoc, having finished her meal, fared better, as her large paws prevented her from sinking; but she stayed close to Hylas, now and then glancing up at him with big Moon-silvered eyes: *Are you sure about this?*

"Did you see that?" whispered Pirra suddenly.

"What? Where?"

"I saw lights, but they went out . . . Over there!"

A dim blue glimmer on the other side of the stream. Hylas had no sooner spotted it than it blinked out.

"Let's go back," said Pirra beside him.

"And go where? If we can just follow this stream, it's bound to lead us out of the marshes—"

"*If* we get that far. If the Marsh Dwellers don't—" With a cry, she lurched against him.

The Crow helmet had been spiked on a fishing spear jammed into a tussock: Pirra had nearly walked right into it. The only trace of the helmet's former owner was a hank of long black warrior braids that had been roughly knotted to its crest. From the other end of these dangled a large, ragged flap of bloody scalp.

"*Now* can we go back?" muttered Pirra. "You don't have to be a Marsh Dweller to know that this means Keep Out!"

"But they meant it for the Crows, not us—"

"And you're quite certain of that, are you?"

After a brief, fierce argument that Pirra won, they

started back for the skeleton tree; but when its white limbs loomed out of the mist, Hylas halted. "We can't go back," he said in an altered voice. "The boat's gone."

Pirra stared at him blankly. "But you tied it up, I saw you."

He licked his lips. "The Marsh Dwellers are Outsiders, Pirra. We won't see them unless they want us to."

Now they had no option but to follow the stream inland.

They hadn't gone far when it narrowed and became nothing more than a willow-choked creek. Hylas felt eyes on him. "Stay close," he murmured. "They're all around, I can feel them."

Out loud, he called softly: "I'm an Outsider too. I come from Mount Lykas, in Lykonia, but my mother was a Marsh Dweller from Messenia. Like you."

No reply. A faint night breeze stirred the reeds and rattled their dry brown heads. The frogs and the night crickets had fallen silent.

"I'm looking for my sister," Hylas went on. "She went missing two summers ago when the Crows attacked our camp. Her name is Issi. I think that means 'frog' in your speech."

Havoc emerged from the mist, making them start. Fish scales glinted on her muzzle and in her chin fur. Rubbing her wet head against Hylas' thigh, she stood and stared into the mist.

Pirra touched his wrist. Her dark eyes were wide in her pale, pointed face. "Don't call again. I don't think they like it."

Havoc raised her head and snuffed the air. Her tail was taut: She'd sensed something upstream.

At that moment, lights flashed behind Hylas' eyes and a burning finger stabbed his temple. He doubled up, clutching his head.

"Hylas!" hissed Pirra. "Is it a vision?"

He tried to answer, but no words came. Everything around him was suddenly sharper and more vivid. He *saw* the swampy green smell rising from the reeds. He heard the suck of a frog's small, sticky feet as it clambered up a stem. And in the midstream, where Pirra saw only weeds, he saw a water spirit rising before him.

At first, she was a nebulous thing of mist and moonlight, but as she rose higher, pearly flakes of light coalesced until she was as clear as the reeds around her. Her green hair floated like weeds, and her cold white eyes slid past Pirra, lingered briefly on Havoc—and pierced Hylas' gaze.

With a gray snarl of a smile, she stretched one long, dripping arm toward him and held out her hand. On her glistening palm sat a tiny tree frog, black in the moonlight. With the other hand, the spirit pointed upstream.

Hylas glanced from the tiny black frog to the radiant webbing between the thin, pointing fingers and in a flash, the spirit's meaning burst upon him. *Frog. Issi. In the marshes.*

He forgot the threat from the Marsh Dwellers. "She's in there!" he cried, crashing through the reeds. *"Issi's in the marshes!"*

"Hylas, come back!" shouted Pirra.

He ignored her, squelching upstream with Havoc in his wake.

Something grabbed his ankle and yanked him into the air; he found himself swinging over the stream by one leg. He was caught in some kind of net.

But the net had also snagged one of Havoc's forepaws, and with a snarl the lioness lashed out with her dagger-sharp claws, ripping apart the tough webbing as if it was gossamer, and dropping Hylas into the stream with a splash.

He surfaced, spitting out waterweed. Havoc had already bounded off into the reeds.

Frightened and furious, Pirra came floundering toward him. "What were you *thinking*? You could have been *killed*!"

Too ashamed to speak, Hylas scrambled onto the bank and hacked at the trip rope around his ankle. It was made of fish skin: thin, but tough. Above him, the sapling, which had been bent double when the trap was set, was now swaying, with the torn net trailing from its crown.

The water spirit had vanished. Frogs *eep-eep*ed mockingly. Reeds rattled with harsh laughter. Pirra was right. If that trap had been spring-loaded with a spear instead of a net, either he or Havoc would be dead by now.

And the marshlights were back, a flickering blue ring all around them—although still there was no one in sight.

Hylas' hand went to his *wedjat* amulet. "Keep your knife

sheathed," he told Pirra softly as they stood back to back.

"I haven't drawn it," she replied. No point. Knives would only make things worse.

"I'm from the mountains of Lykonia," Hylas called to the wavering ring of lights. "But my mother was a Marsh Dweller, like you!"

Silence. But the lights began to close in.

Hylas held up his hands, palm outward in friendship. "I'm looking for my sister. Her name is Issi. She went missing when the Crows—"

The lights blinked out. A fishing spear skewered the mud a hairsbreadth from Hylas' foot. He forced himself to keep still. Pirra sucked in her breath but stood her ground.

A voice spoke from the reeds in a harsh, guttural accent. "We heard you the first time. *Stranger.*"

3

"You are not one of us," spat the Marsh Dweller, emerging from the mist.

Squat and pot-bellied, he wore a tunic of grimy fish skin, and his stumpy limbs were smeared with green mud that stank of swamp. Beneath a fish skin head-binding, his pudgy face was a muddy green. His bulging eyes reminded Pirra of a frog's.

With his fishing spear, he jabbed at the Egyptian amulet on Hylas' chest. "No Outsider has such a thing. No Outsider would fall in a trap as you did. No Outsider would bring the yellow monster who eats our fish. You are not one of us!"

"I'm from Mount Lykas," Hylas said quietly. "But I am an Out—"

"And you!" The Marsh Dweller jabbed at Pirra. "You are no Outsider!"

"I'm Keftian," she said proudly. "The Crows are my enemies."

More Marsh Dwellers appeared, some short and squat, others taller and more slender, but all clad in fish skin and smeared with mud. More spears edged closer.

"Keftians are strangers," said one in the same guttural accent. "We only allow Outsiders in our marshes."

"Pirra's with me," said Hylas. "Where I go, she goes."

Havoc chose that moment to appear among the reeds.

The Marsh Dwellers muttered, some bowing to the lioness as if in awe. They parted to let her through, but when Havoc stood beside Hylas, the ring of spears closed in again.

Hylas put his hand on Havoc's head, willing her to keep calm. "Don't hurt her," he warned the Marsh Dwellers.

"Why would we do that?" retorted an old man. "The yellow monster is why you're still alive!"

"*Fin, feather, and fur,*" said another mysteriously. "You will come with us!"

The Marsh Dwellers didn't seem to have a leader, and Pirra found it hard to tell them apart. All wore fish skin tunics and were smeared in smelly green mud, the women with a reddish strip of wovengrass around their head-bindings, the men with sludgy brown. All regarded her with the same hostile, frog-like stare.

There was something frog-like too in their clammy touch as they stripped her and Hylas of weapons and hustled them onto rafts. Pirra tried not to shudder as fingers probed the crescent-moon scar on her cheek.

Echo was nowhere to be seen and, surprisingly, Havoc had gone off again: Didn't she perceive the Marsh Dwellers as a threat?

Skillfully, they punted through the marshes until they reached a platform of woven reeds, cunningly concealed among willows and dimly lit by rushlights. Hylas and Pirra were made to sit in the middle, and their captors squatted around them with their fishing spears beside them, pointing inward.

Baskets of sludgy green stew appeared. Most of the Marsh Dwellers fell on it, scooping it up with their hands and clicking their sharp gray teeth, while darting baleful glances at their captives. A few sat listlessly, shivering and ignoring the food; Pirra wondered if they were sick.

A basket of stew was plonked in front of her and Hylas. She wrinkled her nose at its fishy stink. "What's in it?" she breathed.

"Don't ask," muttered Hylas, "just eat."

The stew contained some kind of meat, but it smelled awful. Hylas forced down a little. Pirra dipped in a finger, and gagged.

The Marsh Dwellers muttered angrily in their harsh tongue, and Pirra's thoughts flew to the Crow helmet on the spear, with its bloody dangling scalp. She imagined clammy hands seizing her by the hair. She wondered what was in the stew.

The platform lurched, and on leaped Havoc, shaking the wet from her fur. But instead of seizing their spears, the Marsh Dwellers respectfully shuffled aside to make way for her.

The lioness ambled past them and rubbed against

Hylas in greeting, touched noses with Pirra, then gave a cavernous yawn. A woman brought a basket of fish and set it before her with a bow, but Havoc merely sat down and started licking the mud off her paws. From her swollen belly, Pirra guessed that she'd already had all the fish she could eat. Had the Marsh Dwellers been feeding her?

This gave Pirra an idea. *"Fin, feather, and fur,"* she said to the Marsh Dwellers. "What did you mean by that?"

Frog-like eyes blinked in muddy faces. "We know what is *fin*," said a woman.

"We saw the great fish frighten off the Crows," said a man.

"This yellow monster is *fur*. We don't know what is *feather*."

Pirra licked her lips. "I think I do." Raising her arm, she whistled for Echo.

The Marsh Dwellers grabbed their spears. Havoc briefly lifted her head, then went back to licking her paws.

Pirra whistled again.

To her relief, Echo swooped out of the darkness, right over the heads of the Marsh Dwellers, and settled on the leather cuff on her forearm. Unlike Havoc, the falcon was wary of the strangers, hissing and half spreading her wings, ready to fly off at any moment. She caused much muttering, but Pirra couldn't tell if she'd made things better or worse.

An old man spoke to Hylas. "You say your mother was Marsh Dweller. What was her name?"

"I don't know," he replied. "I never knew her."

More muttering: They didn't like that at all.

"I never knew my father either," he added defiantly. "I only know that he was Mountain Clan, and brought shame on his kin by refusing to fight the Crows." A muscle tightened in his jaw. "I'm not like him. Pirra and I have spent two summers fighting them. We came to Messenia to—to get something from them, and to find my sister." His face worked. "I saw something in the marshes, something that told me she's here—"

"The Crows rule everywhere," another man cut in. "They fought the rebels in the north and won. They always win. They have their sacred dagger. They can't be beaten."

Hylas and Pirra exchanged glances. So these people knew about the dagger. "Where is it now?" said Pirra.

Vaguely, a girl waved a muddy hand. "The young Crow lord, he is fighting the last of the rebels in the north."

Pirra didn't look at Hylas. The "young Crow lord" *had* to be Telamon.

The Marsh Dwellers were all talking at once.

"His father, Thestor, is dead . . ."

"Killed in the battle in the north . . ."

"Pharax is in Lykonia, crushing the rebels . . ."

"The old one Koronos has taken over Thestor's stronghold at Lapithos . . ."

"They have the dagger and the favor of the Angry Ones . . ."

Many shuddered and cast fearful glances at the night sky.

A woman spoke in hushed tones. "In the dark of the Moon, Koronos *summoned* Them. On the red peak of Mount Lykas, in the grove of black poplars, he killed black bulls and burnt them. Thus he gained the favor of the Angry Ones . . ."

"Since then," said another, "we hear terrible cries on the wind. We see cloudshadow where there are no clouds. Dread hangs over the reeds like mist, and our people fall victim to the marsh fever . . ."

"Fin, feather, and fur," said a woman. "This is a charm to protect us from the Angry Ones. You are part of this charm. You will stay with us. You will keep us safe."

———

Echo had flown off to perch in a nearby willow. Havoc stood beside Hylas, her great golden eyes intent on the fishing spear pointed at his chest.

Pirra laid a restraining hand on his arm, but Hylas shook it off. "Keeping us here by force," he said hotly, "is no way to beat the Crows, or get rid of the Angry Ones!"

"How do you know?" said a Marsh Dweller stonily.

"You wouldn't survive beyond the marshes," said another. "No one would help you. The Crows will pay well for the hearts of the Outsider with the yellow hair, and the Keftian girl with the scar."

Pirra swallowed. "So they know we're coming?"

"Beyond the marshes," said a man, "you could trust no one! You will stay with us."

"We can't," said Hylas between his teeth. "We're looking for my sister! She's here in the marshes, she must be!"

Muddy faces stared at him blankly.

"She was nine summers old when she went missing," he said with a catch in his voice. "She'd be nearly twelve now. Fair hair, like me—"

"When the Crows came," an old man said, "a few Outsiders fled here from the mountains." He held up four stumpy fingers. "Four boys. No girls."

Hylas continued as if he hadn't spoken. "She's very noisy, always talking, singing, arguing. And always making friends with wild creatures . . . Her favorites are frogs." His voice cracked. "Once, I carved one on the hilt of her knife."

Pirra felt desperately sorry for him. He wanted so much to believe that Issi was still alive.

But the old man was shaking his head. "All boys," he insisted. "No girls."

"She's not dead!" Hylas burst out. "I'd know it if she was, I'd have seen her ghost!"

This horrified them, and their spears drew closer.

Hylas glared at them defiantly. Havoc set back her ears and bared her fangs in a snarl.

"Fin, feather, and fur," Pirra put in quickly. "You said it's some kind of charm. How do you *know?*"

The Marsh Dwellers glanced at one another, as if unsure who should speak. They lowered their spears.

"Last summer," a man began, "when the black ash darkened the marshes, a wisewoman came."

"She cured many who had the marsh fever," said a woman. "Those who get it often die, but she showed us how to make medicine."

"We begged her to stay," said another. "To protect us from the Angry Ones. She refused. We dared not keep her by force. But before she left, she gave us a charm against Them." He touched a grimy little pouch at his neck. Pirra noticed that all the others wore one too.

"The wisewoman did a spirit reading," a woman put in. "She said: *They will come with fin, feather, and fur. They will fight the Evil Ones.*"

Pirra nudged Hylas with her elbow, but he didn't respond. He sat with his head down, clenching and unclenching his fists, still brooding about his sister.

"Where is this wisewoman now?" Pirra demanded.

A woman waved her hand. "She sought some shrine in the mountains to the east. We know she reached it because the Crows thereabouts are plagued by a shadow thief. We think this is a spell of the wisewoman's."

"A shadow thief?" said Pirra with a frown.

"Small as a child, very cunning. It slashes the Crows' waterskins, it spoils their meat. As a sign, it leaves behind a little clay frog."

Hylas' head jerked up. "*What?* Where?"

"With the wisewoman. The shrine they call Dentra."

"What if it's Issi?" cried Hylas. "What if the shadow thief is Issi?"

"But Hylas," Pirra said gently. "Just because Issi loved

frogs, that doesn't mean it's her. Besides, they say it's some kind of spell . . ." Privately, she wondered whether Issi might be dead, and this wisewoman was making use of her spirit.

"Issi used to make clay frogs," insisted Hylas. "It was the only creature she could do!" Then to the Marsh Dwellers: "I have to find this shadow thief, you've got to let us go!"

"No! You will stay with us!"

"You are part of the charm!"

"You protect us from the Angry Ones!"

"Nothing can protect you from the Angry Ones!" he roared.

Echo flew off with a shriek, and Havoc snarled and kneaded the platform with her claws. Pirra put a restraining hand on the lioness' scruff, and shot Hylas a quelling glance.

"This wisewoman," she said to the Marsh Dwellers. "What was her name? Where did she come from?"

"What's that to you?" spat an old woman.

Pirra drew herself up. "I am the daughter of the High Priestess of Keftiu, I've had dealings with wisewomen. Tell me!"

"She came from some island," the woman said sullenly. "The one that blew up and sent the black ash. She said the Crows destroyed it, so now she lives to destroy them."

Pirra's heart was pounding. "Did she have a streak of white here?" She touched the hair at her temple.

The Marsh Dwellers went very still.

"Her name is Hekabi," Pirra declared. "We knew her on Thalakrea. We helped save her people when it blew up."

More muttering.

"Hekabi," added Hylas, "is an extremely powerful wisewoman."

"You wouldn't want to cross her," said Pirra. "She would *definitely* want you to let us go."

<hr />

The Marsh Dwellers squatted at a respectful distance, watching Havoc whiffle in her sleep. The lioness lay sprawled on her back, with Echo perched on her belly, pecking ticks out of her fur.

Hylas and Pirra had withdrawn to a corner of the platform where they could talk without being overheard. The night song of the crickets was changing, and some of the marsh birds were waking up: Soon it would be dawn.

The Marsh Dwellers had at last agreed to guide them out of the marshes. But which way should they go?

"If what they say is right," Pirra said in an undertone, "the dagger's in the north, with Telamon. And if *you're* right, and the shadow thief really is Issi—*if*—then she's in the mountains to the east." She looked at Hylas. "We can't go after them both."

He sat cross-legged, scowling and digging at the platform with his thumbnail. Pirra sensed the warring impulses within him. Must he give up the first potential lead he'd had on his sister in two years, to seek the dagger?

"Maybe we could look for Issi first," she suggested. "And then go after the dagger . . ."

"How could we do that?" he muttered without raising his head. "If we missed our chance at the dagger, how many more rebels would die? And it's my fault the Crows got it back! *My fault!*"

"It's mine too."

"No it's not. I was the one who gave it back."

Pirra's thoughts flew to the battle on the Great River of Egypt. She remembered the knife at her throat, and Telamon yelling at Hylas: *Throw me the dagger, or she dies!*

"Do you regret that?" she said quietly.

"Of course not! But because of what I did, the Crows are rampaging through all Akea, slaughtering rebels." He blew out a long breath. Then he sat up and squared his shoulders. "I've made up my mind. I've got to go after the dagger."

Pirra stiffened. "Don't you mean 'we'?"

He met her eyes. "Pirra . . . I think we need to split up."

She went cold. "I don't understand."

"The Marsh Dwellers will take you east into the mountains, to the peak shrine at Dentra. If you're lucky, you'll find Hekabi there and—and maybe—maybe Issi too. While you're doing that, they'll guide me north. I'll go after the dagger."

"Oh you will, will you?" she said angrily. "A while ago, you said that where you go, I go. What happened to that?"

"Pirra—you know this makes sense."

"No I don't! What I do know is that there's more to this than you're letting on! It's your visions, isn't it? That's what's behind this. You told me in Egypt they've been getting stronger, and now you're worried that they'll be so strong that you won't be able to protect me!"

"And what's wrong with that?" he cried.

"Hylas, I can protect myself, I don't need you to do it for me!"

"Fine! But we're sticking to my plan, whether you like it or not!"

Pirra felt sick with anger and fear and desolation. She couldn't bear the thought of heading off alone with these inscrutable people, into mountains she'd never seen, seeking some child she'd never met, in an alien country, far from her homeland of Keftiu. And all without Hylas.

How can you be so calm? she wanted to yell at him. Don't you realize that if we split up now, we might never see each other again?

But she was too proud to argue, or to beg. "Fine," she said shakily. "I'll look for Issi. You head after the dagger."

4

At first, the she-lion had no idea why the girl was so upset. Why wasn't she talking to the boy anymore? Why weren't they together?

It couldn't be because of the muddy little humans. There was no harm in them, the she-lion had smelled that from the start. In fact, she quite liked them, as they were always giving her fish.

She liked this place too. It was such a *relief* not to be lurching around on the Great Wet, being sick all the time. This place might be a bit soggy, but it had some good rough trees for scratching, and plenty of reeds for hiding in; wet for splashing about, and lots of lovely squelchy mud for cooling her pads. Best of all, it had no bad crow-humans, or dogs.

And so much prey! Frogs, ducks, herons. Small sideways-scuttling creatures that reminded her of spiders, but had interestingly crunchy shells . . . And *lots* of fish. Some were almost as big as she was, and lurked at the bottom of the wet, while the smaller ones let themselves be caught by the muddy humans in little grass sacks that were great fun to rip open.

Yes, this place would make an excellent range for her pride. So why didn't any of the others want to stay?

As usual, the falcon was making her views extremely plain. Instead of roosting in a tree as she usually did rather boringly every Dark, she kept starting awake and glaring at the Up, then angrily shaking out her feathers and settling down again. This gave the she-lion a squirmy feeling in her belly, because it reminded her of the shadow that had sped across the Up just after they'd reached land—and *that* reminded her of the terrible spirits who used to haunt her very worst sleeps when she was a cub.

The she-lion *hated* thinking about the terrible spirits, and she hoped They would never ever come back. In fact, They were the best reason of all for staying in this safe, soggy place among the reeds.

But instead, the boy and the girl were heading for the *edge* of the reeds—*and they were going in different directions.*

Like all humans, they were noisy and slow, so it was easy to keep track of them. As the Light grew stronger, the she-lion kept bounding ahead to catch the smells from the land beyond the reeds—grass, hare, deer, mountain— then trotting back to check on the rest of the pride. Each time she did, she was alarmed to find that the gap between the boy and the girl had grown bigger.

The next time she went back, they were very far apart indeed. The boy was trudging one way with a small group of muddy little humans; the girl was already a long way away from him and heading for the mountains, in the company of a new pair of mud-people, who'd been waiting for her at the edge of the reeds.

The she-lion didn't understand this at all. Once again, she went and found the boy, and rubbed against his legs, rumbling deep in her throat, to ask for reassurance.

The boy bent and touched his forehead to hers, talking to her in human talk. His voice was low and rough with sadness. Then he pushed her away and spoke more sharply, pointing at the mountains, where the girl and the falcon had gone. Then, without looking back, he walked off in the other direction.

The she-lion bounded after him and biffed him playfully around the hind legs, knocking him over and batting his head lightly between her forepaws. He pushed her off and scrambled to his feet. Again he spoke sharply. Again he pointed at the mountains.

This must be some new kind of game. The she-lion leaped at him and flung her forepaws around his neck, telling him in groany lion talk how much she loved being with him.

He pushed her away quite hard (for him), and this time when he pointed at the mountains, he *shouted,* and she was astonished to hear anger in his voice—although with sadness underneath.

Suddenly, the truth bit the she-lion on the nose. *The boy didn't want her to go with him. He wanted her to follow the girl and the falcon into the mountains. The pride was splitting up!*

The she-lion sat on her haunches and gazed up at him in bewilderment. She forgot about being full-grown, and whimpered like a cub. No no no, you *can't* break up the pride!

The boy was taking big ragged breaths and rubbing his muzzle with his forepaw. Then he turned and stumbled away.

Mewing softly, the she-lion watched him walk off under the trees. He didn't look back.

Still mewing, she padded in a circle. She trotted after him. She stopped. She leaped onto a rock and watched until she could no longer see him and the wind had chased away the last of his scent. She went on watching, but he didn't return. He really was *gone*.

The she-lion felt a gnawing emptiness, as if she hadn't eaten for many Lights and Darks—only this hurt far worse than that.

She couldn't believe that the boy had actually left. She kept hoping it was another game, and that soon she would hear his funny, breathless human laugh as he came crashing through the undergrowth, calling for her . . .

But though she stayed on her rock, patiently waiting while the Great Lion rose higher in the Up, all she heard was the chatter of birds, and the trees talking to the wind.

What had she done wrong? Why didn't he want her anymore?

At last, she leaped down from the rock and started plodding after the scent of the girl and her two muddy little humans.

The Great Lion rose higher in the Up, and the she-lion grew dusty and hot as she headed into the hills. She plodded past the scattered lairs of humans, where there were tempting pigs and goats. She climbed through forests full of deer, and the rich hot smells of boar. She ignored them all. The scent-trails of the girl and the muddy humans streamed over her nose, and she tracked them without eagerness, for she had nowhere else to go— but they were the *wrong* scents and the wrong humans, because they weren't the boy.

This was not how things should be. *Why* had he sent her away? Why didn't the girl go and *fetch* him?

Everything was tangled and wrong. They were a *pride,* and a pride must never, ever split up. A pride must stay *together.*

Hylas heard the whinny of a horse and dropped to his knees in the bracken. From somewhere below came the sound of men's voices and a whiff of woodsmoke.

Silently, he made his way down the slope, moving from one pine trunk to the next. He peered through the bracken.

The Crow camp lay about thirty paces below. By the look of it, his Marsh Dweller guides had been right, and Telamon had left most of his warriors rounding up the defeated rebels in the north, while he headed south with a handful of men.

Did Telamon have the dagger? Or was it in the Crows' ancestral stronghold of Lapithos, on the other side of the mountains? Hylas had no idea—but he knew Telamon. Telamon was arrogant, and growing more so. Having regained the dagger in Egypt, he wouldn't want to give it up. Could he have found some way to keep it from Koronos or Pharax? If so, he might have it with him now.

The Crows had camped for the night on a shoulder of the hillside. To Hylas' left, he saw chestnut trees bordering a stream, and a trail leading downhill into the next valley. Two Crow warriors in black rawhide armor sat cooling their feet in the water, while three more tended a cooking pot hung over a fire. Twenty paces downstream, four others tended a second fire. All of them looked dusty and exhausted.

On the other side of the camp, to Hylas' right, the hillside fell away sharply into a gully, and at the edge of this, a pine tree shaded the camp's only tent. It was of scarlet wool, and clearly the tent of a chieftain: It had to be Telamon's.

Immediately below Hylas, two chariot horses, tethered to stakes, were cropping grass near the disassembled pieces of a splendidly gilded chariot. Hylas smiled grimly. A chariot and horses weren't much use in the foothills of mountains, but they were costly and rare, and Telamon had always cared immensely about appearances. What was it to him if his men had to look after the beasts *and* lug the pieces of his chariot over the mountains? Doubtless the moment they reached the plains, he would have it reassembled, so that he could enjoy driving his high-stepping horses before his men.

A scrawny, anxious-looking slave scuttled out of the tent bearing a large bronze basin, which he ran to fill at the stream. Shortly afterward, the tent flaps were flung back and Telamon himself strode out.

He was even more magnificently dressed than when Hylas had seen him in Egypt, three moons before. From the top of his boar's-tusk helmet swung a glossy black horsetail, and his armor was no longer rawhide, but burnished bronze. Strips of gleaming bronze covered his kilt; bronze greaves protected his shins, and bronze arm-guards his forearms. His figured breastplate dazzled in the late-afternoon Sun, and his shoulder-guards were so broad that he resembled a legendary hero from the past. On a hauberk across his chest hung a sword with a gilded hilt. And yet, Hylas noticed with a jolt, from the scarlet sheath at Telamon's belt jutted a knife's plain, unadorned hilt.

Hylas' heart began to race. Surely that was the dagger of Koronos?

It didn't take him long to work out a plan. When everyone was asleep, he would sneak down the slope and prepare his escape route, by tying his rope to that pine tree and letting it down the gully, so that it would be ready when needed. After that, he would stampede the horses—and pray to every god he could think of that Telamon and his men would go after the beasts, or at least be distracted for long enough to let him snatch the dagger and make off down the gully.

It wasn't much of a plan, not least because he wasn't *entirely* sure that the rope would be long enough to reach the bottom of the gully. Also, Telamon might take the dagger with him when he went after the horses, instead of leaving it in the tent. But it was the best Hylas could come up with, and he knew he had to act now. If Telamon joined up again with the rest of his forces, or if he returned to Lapithos, the dagger would be out of reach.

"Keep the fires burning all night," Telamon barked at his men. "I want a brazier in my tent, torches staked around camp, and two sentries on duty till dawn."

The men's shoulders slumped. "But my lord," said one. "There's not many rebels in these parts. And to do all that, we'd have to gather lots more wood—"

"I don't care," Telamon said coldly. "Get it done."

"Yes, my lord."

Turning on his heel, Telamon stalked back to his tent. Scowling and grumbling under their breath, his men heaved themselves to their feet.

Hylas settled down in the bracken to wait for dusk.

The song of the crickets slowed, and as the Sun went down, Hylas watched the valley gradually fill with shadow. The sky was overcast. Good. The last thing he wanted was moonlight.

In the mountains, thunder growled, and with a pang he thought of Havoc and Pirra, far to the south. But he'd been *right* to send them away, he knew that. Staying together would have been far too dangerous.

Below him, the Crow warriors were trudging back to camp, bearing armfuls of firewood. Wearily, they fed the fires and planted torches around camp, then lugged a bronze brazier and a large pile of sticks into Telamon's tent. After that, they settled around their fires and fell on their evening meal. The oniony smell of gruel drifted up the slope.

It was almost dark when one of the warriors stood up, yawning, and wandered over to the horses. The black horse whickered a greeting as the man untied its tether, but the brown one with the dark mane set back its ears and lunged at him with its yellow teeth bared.

"Get away, you monster!" snarled the warrior, snatching a stick and striking the horse a vicious blow on the head. Then he dragged the docile black one over to the water, and waited impatiently while it drank. In the evening hush, Hylas heard the beast's long, slow, grateful slurps.

After returning the black horse to its grazing spot, the warrior hefted his stick and warily approached the brown one. It set back its ears, rolling its eyes at the stick, and as he stooped to undo its tether, it nipped him on the thigh.

Bellowing with rage, the warrior struck the horse across the eyes. It squealed and reared. "Then go thirsty!" shouted the man as he stomped back to the fire, amid jeering and laughter from his comrades.

The brown horse was tugging at its stake in vain, and eyeing the stream that was so far out of reach. The sound of the water must be agonizing.

Something about the horse's bony nose and scarred flanks jogged Hylas' memory. Jinx, he thought. Yes, I remember you, your name is Jinx. And the black one's name is Smoke.

Two summers before, these horses had belonged to Telamon's father, Thestor, the Chieftain of Lykonia.

Telamon had "borrowed" them and the chariot without his permission, and driven to Hylas' rescue. He'd helped Hylas escape. Back then, he and Telamon had been best friends.

For a moment, Hylas' spirits plunged. They'd been *friends* . . . Telamon used to slip away from his father's stronghold of Lapithos, and he and Hylas and Issi would range the slopes of Mount Lykas, stealing honey from bees' nests, and getting into scrapes. They'd built their first raft together, and learned to swim. Telamon had saved Hylas from an angry bull, and Hylas had hauled Telamon out of the cave of an irritated lioness.

Where had all that gone? How could it be that Thestor, who for years had kept Lykonia peaceful by having nothing to do with his kinsmen of the House of Koronos—that Thestor was dead in battle, and his son Telamon had become a cruel, arrogant, murderous young warrior? How was it *possible*?

Night fell. Bats flickered overhead. Hylas struggled to stay awake.

Below him, the horses stood dozing with their heads down. The two sentries leaned on their spears by the fires. The other warriors had rolled themselves in their cloaks and fallen asleep.

Telamon's slave slept on the ground outside the front of the tent, whose red walls glowed, lit from within by the brazier. Hylas made out Telamon's dark silhouette, pacing up and down inside. Now and then, Telamon raised a drinking cup to his lips, pausing often to refill it from a jug on the ground; and from time to time, he fiddled with something at his wrist. Hylas guessed that was his sealstone. When he was a boy, Telamon used to fiddle with it when he was nervous.

Was he nervous now? He'd beaten the rebels, so why did he still fear attack? Was that why he'd had his men pitch his tent at the edge of the gully? To prevent attack from that side? Was that why he'd insisted on all those torches planted around camp, and on having a brazier burning in his tent, even though the night was warm?

Midnight passed, and still Telamon paced. Hylas' legs felt stiff and cramped. It was hard to keep his eyes open.

At last, the dark figure inside the tent stopped pacing. Hylas saw Telamon kneel and draw something from his belt. Was it the dagger? Now he was lifting the lid off some kind of box and laying something inside, then carefully replacing the lid. Hylas was wide awake. He thought of the narrow box of polished wood in which the Crows had kept the dagger, on Thalakrea.

By the stream, the warriors still slept, and the sentries dozed at their posts. The Crow camp was dark, only fitfully lit by the torches.

Finally, Telamon settled himself on the ground, and after much tossing and turning, he too lay still.

Soundlessly, Hylas started down the slope. First, he would secure his escape by tying the rope to that tree, then he'd stampede the horses.

Passing downwind of them so as not to wake them too early, he found the dismantled chariot, where he hid his waterskin and the bag of provisions that his Marsh Dweller guides had given him before they'd headed back to the marshes. Over his shoulder, he slung their parting gift, a coil of tough fish skin rope.

By the stream, a warrior muttered. Hylas ducked behind the chariot wheels. The warrior grunted in his sleep and turned over. His grunts didn't seem to have woken the sentries; and no noises came from Telamon's tent, except the occasional snore.

Hylas crept behind the tent to the pine tree at the edge of the gully. It was surrounded by clumps of prickly broom; pushing through this, he tied one end of the rope around the tree trunk, then quietly uncoiled the rest down the gully.

Suddenly, a cry of terror rent the air.

Hylas dived into the broom bushes.

That cry had been Telamon's. Hylas heard warriors running toward the tent—"You all right, my lord?"—and the slave's tentative "My lord?"

"Go back to your posts, all of you!" shouted Telamon from inside the tent. To Hylas, crouching behind it, he sounded terrifyingly close.

"Yes, my lord," muttered the slave.

Not daring to breathe, Hylas listened to the warriors' footsteps retreating, and the slave settling down again at the front of the tent. He heard Telamon muttering as he threw more wood on the brazier, then throwing himself once more onto the ground.

Finally, all went quiet.

Hylas pushed his head out of the bushes. Yes, still quiet.

He was about to crawl out when he heard footsteps coming around the other side of the tent. He froze. The footsteps stopped. Whoever it was must be standing no more than a few paces from where he knelt.

"This can't go on," said Telamon. *"This can't go on!"*

6

"This can't go on," muttered Telamon. "You have to be *strong* . . ."

Hidden in the bushes, Hylas heard Telamon's voice grow louder, then softer as he paced the edge of the gully. Telamon came to a halt, appallingly close. Hylas held his breath. His life depended on a few branches of prickly broom, and on keeping utterly still.

But Telamon was oblivious to his surroundings. "It wasn't your *fault*," he told himself. "You didn't *do* anything!"

It was too dark to see him clearly, but Hylas saw the sheen of sweat on his forehead, and the dark circles under his eyes.

Something tickled Hylas' foot. Spider? Scorpion? He fought to keep still.

"Not your *fault*," repeated Telamon, twisting his sealstone as he paced.

Only a spider. Silently, Hylas breathed out.

This time when Telamon drew near, Hylas saw that it wasn't a sealstone he was twisting, but a ring on his forefinger, a broad band of dull gray metal that he was grinding into his flesh. Hylas had seen Koronos wearing a ring like that once. It was made of iron. Hylas had learned about iron from Akastos, the mysterious wanderer who'd crossed his path several times over the years, and for whom he'd worked in the smithy on Thalakrea.

"Iron," Akastos had told him, "is the rarest of metals because it falls from the stars. You can use it to ward off the Angry Ones—but not for long; against Them, nothing works for long."

But why, wondered Hylas, does Telamon wear iron, when the Crows *worship* the Angry Ones?

"It wasn't your *fault*," Telamon told himself a third time.

But it was, and he knew it. Three moons ago in Egypt, he had left his own kinswoman to die. Hylas would never forget Alekto's screams as she clung to her sinking boat, and the crocodiles gliding toward her like the rays of some evil green star . . .

Telamon could have saved her, but he'd chosen not to. Was that why he couldn't sleep? Did he live in terror of the Angry Ones, the dreadful spirits of vengeance who hunt those who have murdered their kin?

Suddenly, pain stabbed Hylas' temples, so fierce that he nearly cried out. Lights flashed behind his eyes. He put his hand to his mouth to keep from retching.

The sickness subsided, but this time when he peered through the branches, what he saw nearly stopped his heart. His skin prickled. He felt the hairs on his forearms rise.

Telamon was still muttering and staring down at the ring he kept twisting around and around—and before him, on the empty air above the gully, stood his father's ghost.

It wavered, as if Hylas saw it through rippling water, but he knew it was Thestor. He'd seen him once, and he'd never forgotten, because it was the first time he'd seen Telamon too. A cold winter's day: Hylas had been rescuing Issi from a fight with some village boys, when Telamon and his father, out hunting, had stopped to watch . . .

It was Thestor's ghost, but shockingly altered from what he'd been in life. One side of its body was a horror of black blood and mangled flesh, and its heavy, handsome features were haggard with despair.

Perhaps sensing something, Telamon raised his head. "Who's there?" he whispered, gazing unseeing into the dark.

The ghost glared at his son with dreadful urgency.

"Who's *there*?" hissed Telamon.

The ghost's gaze never wavered, but a look of shame convulsed the haggard features. Slowly, it shook its head. Then it raised its hand and pointed at the sky. Hylas found it horrible that Telamon should be staring straight at his father's spirit, and yet he could not see.

Again, the spirit shook its ruined head. Then it turned and slowly limped away across the void.

"My lord, you called?" whispered a voice, making Hylas jump.

Telamon too spun around with a start.

His slave was peering nervously around the corner of the tent: fortunately for Hylas, the side farthest from him.

With a shaky hand, Telamon wiped the sweat from his face. "What d'you want?" he said thickly.

"My lord, you're ill! I can mix more wine, or—or there's poppy juice left . . ."

"Poppy juice," mumbled Telamon. "Yes . . . I'm tired, that's all. I just need to sleep."

Hylas watched them disappear around the far side of the tent. He heard them go back inside. He breathed out. He felt hollow and sick, and his head was throbbing.

And in the darkness over the gully, he could see Thestor's ghost growing fainter and fainter as it limped off over the empty air.

An owl called from the gully. The pine tree creaked in the night wind. And still Hylas stayed in the bushes, waiting for Telamon and his slave to go to sleep.

At last, all was silent, and Hylas crawled out. Somehow, he had to put the vision of Thestor behind him and get on with his plan: Stampede the horses and hope against hope that in the confusion, he could steal the dagger and escape.

Dawn wasn't far off, but the camp was in darkness, except for the glimmer of torches staked at intervals. Keeping to the shadows, Hylas retrieved his waterskin and food bag from behind the chariot, then stole to the nearest torch and wrenched it from the ground.

The horses had been asleep, but as he crept behind them, the black one, Smoke, smelled the fire and woke with a start. Jinx was already snorting and rolling his eyes, but he seemed more intent on nipping Hylas than on running away. Hylas yanked the slipknots from their tethers and brandished the torch before their noses, waving his arms and hissing.

That did it. Smoke squealed in terror, Jinx reared, then both went thundering through camp. The whole place sprang awake: sentries shouting, their comrades blearily grabbing weapons, Telamon and his slave bursting from the tent. Now all were rushing after the horses, which had gone hurtling down the trail that led to the next valley.

"After them!" yelled Telamon. "I'll have any man flogged who dares come back before we've caught them!"

As soon as they were gone, Hylas raced for the tent. Inside, it was stiflingly hot, the brazier redly aglow, but there lay the wooden box, half covered by Telamon's black cloak, which in his haste he'd flung aside. Hylas threw off the lid and grabbed the dagger.

Or rather, he grabbed *a* dagger—but not the dagger of Koronos. What he held in his hand was nothing but a cheap copper knife.

Suddenly, he felt eyes on him. He threw himself sideways, and Telamon's spear skewered the ground where he'd been kneeling a heartbeat before. Telamon had set a trap, and he'd walked right into it.

"How'd you know I was here?" panted Hylas, scrambling to his feet and putting the brazier between them.

"I didn't; I guessed," said Telamon, wrenching his spear free.

"But you laid your trap with the knife *before* the horses ran off," said Hylas as they circled the brazier, feinting this way and that. "You couldn't have known I was here!"

Another thrust with the spear, which again Hylas dodged. "I didn't know *when* you'd come," panted Telamon, "but I knew that you would. I've been making that little show with the knife every night."

As they circled the brazier, Hylas' mind raced. He was armed with his own knife and the inferior copper one, while Telamon had a vicious bronze sword and a heavy bronze thrusting spear; he was also a year older and a trained warrior. And his men might have come back with him, they might be surrounding the tent right now.

And yet . . . It would be unlike Telamon to seek help from his men: He would want the glory of killing the Outsider for himself. And that meant he'd probably left his men going after the horses, and returned alone.

"Aren't you going to squeal for help?" taunted Hylas, to make sure.

Telamon jabbed his spear at Hylas' chest. He'd moved clumsily—the point only nicked Hylas' wrist, but the pain was enough to make him drop his knife.

"I don't need help," snarled Telamon, kicking it out of Hylas' reach. Now all he had was the copper knife.

"So where's the real dagger?" said Hylas. "With your grandfather Koronos, at Lapithos?"

Telamon didn't reply, but something in his face told Hylas that he'd guessed right. "Poor Telamon," he sneered. "Your grandfather didn't trust you with the real dagger, he sent you off as a decoy with a fake! Not very heroic, is it, being pushed around by your elders!"

Once more, Telamon lunged with his spear. Hylas sidestepped, grabbing the shaft and twisting it upward. Telamon hissed, but clung on. Wrenching the spear from Hylas' grip, he thrust his sword at his chest. Again his aim was off, and the point grazed Hylas' forearm. Hylas cried out, and the copper knife went flying. Telamon flicked it out of reach with his spear and forced his enemy back behind the brazier.

Weaponless, Hylas grabbed a burning brand, scanning his side of the tent for what else he could use. A jug of wine, a bronze scraper, and a jar of oil—doubtless Telamon's slave used that for cleaning dust from his master's limbs— and a man-high shield of thick oxhide that looked too heavy to be much help.

Telamon made another clumsy jab with the spear, which Hylas dodged, and Telamon stumbled and nearly lost his footing. Hylas gave a breathless laugh. "Not too steady on your feet, are you? What's wrong, all that wine and poppy juice fuddling your wits?"

"Nothing I can't handle," spat Telamon. "I swore once that I'd kill you and feed your heart to the dogs—"

"And maybe then the Angry Ones will stop haunting you, eh?" Hylas shot back.

Telamon blinked.

"That's why you wear that iron ring, isn't it? They're after you because of what you did in Egypt—"

"I did *nothing*!" cried Telamon. "It just *happened*, it was the will of the gods! Alekto fell overboard—"

"Is that what you told Pharax and Koronos? We both know it's a lie, though, don't we? I was there, I saw! You could have saved her, but you left her to the crocodiles! You can't fool the Angry Ones, Telamon. You can't fool your Ancestors, either. Your father knows what you did!"

Telamon lurched to a halt.

"I saw his ghost," panted Hylas. "He was right there in front of you while you were pacing up and down on the edge of the gully!"

"You're making that up," said Telamon, scarcely moving his lips. But he stood rooted to the ground, his weapons forgotten in his hands.

"He shook his head in *shame*, Telamon. He turned his back on you and walked away—"

"You're making it up!" cried Telamon.

Hylas caught the sound of running feet in the distance: The warriors were coming back. "Then where's his seal-stone?" he countered, playing for time and wondering desperately what to try next. "He was bloody and mangled down one side, and his sealstone was missing from his wrist. You told me once that he never took it off, that he'd sworn he would take it with him to his tomb."

Telamon's face had gone gray. "He lost it in battle . . . Nobody knew that . . . How could you know?"

"I told you," said Hylas, "I saw his ghost! He pointed at the sky, Telamon . . . he *knows* the Angry Ones are after you! He knows what you did—and so do They!"

Telamon gave a strangled cry. At the same moment, Hylas dashed the burning brand at him, then seized the heavy shield in both hands and bashed Telamon over the head. Half stunned, Telamon sank to his knees. Shouts outside: Another instant, and the warriors would burst in. Snatching his knife and sheathing it, Hylas grabbed the oil jar, splashed oil all around the tent, and tipped over the brazier. The oil-spattered wool caught fire at once, and as the warriors burst in, Hylas kicked down the tent pole and wriggled out the other end.

Howls from within as the blazing tent collapsed upon the Crows. Hylas was already scrambling down the rope, into the gully. Above him he heard yells and scuffling . . . He pictured his erstwhile friend trapped in the blazing tent. He's not your friend anymore, he told himself grimly. He'd have skewered you like a hog if he'd had the chance.

Glancing up, he glimpsed a warrior at the edge of the gully. The warrior crouched down and started hacking at the rope.

Hylas slid farther, skinning his palms and bumping against rocks and thornscrub. He grabbed a sapling. An instant later, the warrior cut the rope, which came tumbling down upon him. Somehow, he clung to the sapling. Then he half climbed, half fell the rest of the way, ending up in a clump of bracken.

The Crows' shouts faded as he crashed blindly through the dark, clutching his *wedjat* amulet and praying to the Lady of the Wild Things that he would find the mouth of the gully, instead of blundering into a dead end.

7

"We haven't got him yet, my lord!" panted the warrior.

"I can see that," snapped Telamon. "The question is *why*, when there are nine of you and only one of him!"

"Er—six, my lord, the others are still looking for the horses—"

"Why haven't they found them?"

The warrior swallowed. "They caught the black one, my lord. The other's still missing."

"Then they'd better catch it, hadn't they? And you'd better catch the Outsider!"

When the man had run off again, Telamon went back to rifling through the charred remains of his tent. His slave was on his knees and, like him, covered in soot. At some stage during the fight with Hylas, or the struggle to escape the fire, Telamon's iron ring had slipped off his finger. He *had* to find it. His mind shied away from what would happen if he did not.

It was still dark, and above him, the cloudy sky seemed filled with vast, writhing shadows. Without the ring, he had no protection from the terror that came in the night.

He thought of his father's ghost . . . Hylas *must* have been lying. It wasn't possible that Thestor's spirit was not at peace: that he was *ashamed* of what his son had become . . .

"My lord?" His slave was staring up at him in puzzlement.

Telamon flushed. Had he spoken out loud? "Keep looking!" he barked. "If you don't find it, I'll have you flogged!"

"Y-yes, my lord."

What were you *doing*, scrabbling around in the soot? thought Telamon as he strode over to wash at the stream. That's not how a chieftain acts!

His head was pounding from that blow with the shield, and the burns on his shins hurt savagely, despite his slave's goosefat salve. He felt bleary and sick from too much wine and poppy juice.

In a tree by the stream, a dark shape stirred.

Telamon lurched to a halt.

Another gust of wind stirred the branches. He breathed out. "The wind," he murmured. "It was only the wind."

A leathery *thwap* nearby. He cringed, picturing vast wings swooping toward him.

More *thwaps*, louder this time—and among the ruins of the tent, his slave stood up, shaking out his master's singed cloak with vigorous snaps, then began folding it up.

"*Leave that!*" bellowed Telamon. "I *told* you, the only thing that matters is finding the *ring!*"

Grabbing a torch, he ran to the edge of the stream and jabbed the stake in the mud. Squatting on his haunches, he passed a trembling hand across his face. "You *must* get hold of yourself," he whispered. "You are a chieftain. You will be the greatest chieftain of them all!"

But he knew these were merely words. In his mind, he kept reliving the moment when he'd first begun to suspect that the Angry Ones might be after him.

It had been on Mount Lykas, just below the tallest peak, at the Place of the Ancestors. Midnight, at the dark of the Moon, in the murmurous grove of black pines that guarded the entrance to the tomb of the House of Koronos.

Long ago, the Ancestors had cut the narrow tomb into the mountain. Two moons before, its doorway had been broken open to admit Thestor's body; and now Koronos had ordered his grandson Telamon and Pharax, his last surviving son, to return, and help him perform the rite that would summon the Angry Ones and gain Their help in the attack that would crush the rebels forever.

The sacrifice itself was a blur in Telamon's mind. The Angry Ones are drawn to darkness and burned things: He remembered the hiss as the torches were quenched. He remembered his kinsmen's chanting and the reek of burned meat; the bitter smell of the ash on his cheeks, the coppery sweetness of the blood and wine in his mouth. Then all at once, he'd heard the rush of enormous wings.

Before, when his grandfather had made sacrifices, the

Angry Ones had swept low, and then off into the night—but not this time. This time, three vast dark shadows had dropped to the ground not ten paces from where Telamon stood.

He'd caught the stink of the spirits' charred flesh. He'd seen the darkness thicken into dreadful snake-like necks and raw red mouths like gaping wounds. He'd heard the scrabble of claws and a horrible, insistent snuffling. He'd stood rigid with horror: Was it possible that They were sniffing him out in the dark?

The next moment, fiery red eyes had fixed on his. His thoughts had darted in panic. Did They know what he'd done?

The Angry Ones come from the Chaos before the gods, and They hunt those who have murdered their kin. They never give up, and They don't care who gets in their way. You might ward Them off for a while by chewing buckthorn leaves, or muttering an ancient charm; you might disguise yourself and flee your homeland. But sooner or later, They will find you, and scorch your spirit to madness . . .

At last Telamon had torn himself free from those horrifying eyes. He'd staggered over to Pharax. Gasping with terror, he'd clutched his uncle's arm. "They're coming for me!" he'd wheezed.

Coldly, Pharax had shaken him off. "Be a man," he'd said in his hollow, stony voice. "Or are you *afraid* of the *dark*?"

When Telamon had looked again, the dreadful, twisting

shadows were gone; and shortly afterward, the rite had ended, and they'd taken the path down to Lapithos. But for Telamon, everything had changed. An appalling suspicion had taken root in his mind: that the spirits of vengeance might be after *him*.

Since then, he hadn't been able to eat or sleep—except when he drank too much wine or poppy juice. He dreaded the terror that haunted his dreams.

And now his own father's ghost had come to him. Hylas hadn't been lying, Telamon knew that in his heart. Thestor had come to confirm Telamon's suspicions. The Angry Ones *knew* what he'd done. They knew that he'd left his own kinswoman in the churning red horror in the river, to be eaten by crocodiles . . . And now They were after him.

An owl hooted. Telamon bared his teeth in a grimace. He plunged his grimy hands into the stream.

The water was cold, and he welcomed that. As he watched the soot lifting from his skin and floating away down the hillside, he felt a little steadier.

It was peaceful here. The night air was sharp with the scent of mint. Ferns were cool against his calves. Somewhere, a nightingale sang.

Without warning, he found himself fighting back tears. There had been nightingales outside his chamber at Lapithos when he was a boy; they used to keep him awake at night. At that time, he hadn't even known he *had* a grandfather Koronos, or that Koronos was High Chieftain of Mycenae, far to the north. And Hylas had been his friend, and his father was still alive.

Angrily, Telamon rubbed his hands to wash off the last of the soot. He splashed his face, dunked his head, and wrung out his long warrior braids. He cupped his hands and drank. The water was so cold it set his teeth on edge. It cleared his head wonderfully.

"Found it, my lord!" His slave came racing across to him and pressed the iron ring into his palm.

Telamon slipped the ring on his finger and made a fist. He drew deep, steady breaths. He felt stronger and much more in control. "Good," he said. "Very good.

"Good," he repeated, watching his slave hurry back to the ruined tent, to salvage more of his belongings. Again, Telamon cupped his hands and drank. Then he rose to his feet and squared his shoulders.

"You are a chieftain," he told himself out loud. "*You* are in control. It wasn't your fault that Alekto died. You didn't kill her, it was the crocodiles: *It was the will of the gods*. The Angry Ones know that. Alekto died so that *you* could get the dagger back—so that *you* could be the savior of your clan."

With new resolve, he strode up and down beneath the chestnut trees. His terror was gone, he felt full of resolution and purpose. His sleepless nights were in the past. At daybreak, he would rally his men and go after Hylas. The Outsider couldn't hide for long, not against warriors who'd grown up in these Messenian hills.

When Hylas was dead, he, Telamon, would rejoin the rest of his men. He would order Ilarkos to lead them across the mountains into Lykonia, and help Pharax defeat the last of the rebels; then he would defy his grandfather's orders and head back to Lapithos. No more being told what to do: He would confront Koronos—and take the dagger for his own.

With a flash of insight, he realized now why the Angry Ones had come after him on that night in the grove of black pines: *They had scented weakness.*

"Yes," he murmured, "that's what it was."

But once he'd taken the dagger for his own, everything would change. *He* would be High Chieftain of all Akea. The Angry Ones would leave him in peace.

And he would never be frightened again.

8

"How many more days till we find Hekabi?" Pirra said wearily, dumping her gear on the ground and easing her aching shoulders.

The two Marsh Dweller boys went on pitching camp as if she hadn't spoken.

"Well, how many?" she said crossly. "Two? Three? A whole moon?"

The younger one threw her a stony glance; the older one shrugged. "Couple of days," he grunted.

"*Thank* you," she said sarcastically.

They'd been trudging into the foothills for three days, and she still didn't know their names. They'd met her at the edge of the marshes the evening after Hylas had gone: two sullen boys, one younger than her, the other about her age; both plainly resentful at having to guide a girl.

In her head, she'd nicknamed the older boy Weasel because he looked like one, and the younger boy Stone, as he never said a word. They were scrawny for Marsh Dwellers, and wore the usual fish skin tunics, head-bindings, and smelly green mud. That mud made the whites of their eyes alarmingly bright when they stared at her—which they did a lot.

Still, they seemed to know the way to the peak shrine at Dentra, and they'd led her confidently along hidden trails that followed a river northeast toward the mountains. As the mountains loomed closer, Pirra's spirits sank still further. Those peaks were jagged and forbidding—and yet that was where Hylas had grown up. It made her feel as if she'd never really known him.

How could you leave me, Hylas, she berated him in her head as she watched her two sullen guides gathering firewood. Why did you have to go off on your own?

Somehow, it made it even worse that he'd left before she'd been handed over to Weasel and Stone. If only you could see how horrible they are, she wanted to tell him. Then you'd be sorry!

She wasn't the only one who was missing him, either. Echo was listless, ignoring the birds that thronged the forest, and Havoc hadn't gone hunting since the day he'd left. The light was gone from her great golden eyes, and her fur had become dull and bedraggled. She didn't understand why he'd sent her away.

The boy whom Pirra had nicknamed Stone treated Havoc and Echo with wary respect, but Weasel was *terrified* of them. Earlier, Havoc had pushed past him to reach Pirra, and the Marsh Dweller boy had whimpered: "Get it *away* from me!" Showing fear was the worst thing he could have done, and soon afterward, Havoc had lain in wait for him around a bend, and batted his ankles to trip him up.

"She won't hurt you," Pirra had told the squealing boy as she'd struggled to push the lioness off him. "She's just miserable, that's why she's playing up. Havoc, *stop* it!" But ever since, Weasel would flinch if Havoc so much as yawned.

They'd halted for the night at a place where the river widened into a small pool of clear green water. Not a bad campsite, Pirra thought grudgingly. Sparrows chirped in the pines and the walnut trees, and yellow irises swayed among the reeds fringing the banks. A fig tree was laden with sweet golden figs, and she spotted bushes with ripe raspberries. Raspberries were Hylas' favorites. If only he were here now.

Stone flung down an armful of firewood, making her jump. To be helpful, she offered to gather some more, and was rewarded with his unblinking stare.

"Why doesn't he ever speak?" she asked Weasel irritably.

"He can't," muttered the older boy.

"But why?"

"He had a bad time with the Crows."

"What do you mean?"

"How would I know, when he can't speak?" snapped Weasel. "Maybe he seen stuff, maybe they beat him up. Some people went mad after the Crows got hold of them, so he's luckier than most!"

"I'm sorry," said Pirra. "Whatever happened to him, it must have been awful."

Both boys stared at her, then went back to breaking up kindling. She felt more lonely and dejected than ever.

When the silence had gone on long enough, she said: "When we find Hekabi, do you think the shadow thief will still be with her?"

"Why are you looking for the shadow thief?" said Weasel without raising his head.

"Because the shadow thief might be Hylas' sister."

"Who's Hylas?" said Weasel with a frown.

Pirra reminded herself that neither Weasel nor Stone had ever seen Hylas, who'd left for the mountains well before they'd taken charge of her at the edge of the marshes. "Hylas," she said, "is my—he's my friend. He's looking for his sister—"

"Why can't he look for her himself?"

"Because he has to fight the Crows."

"Are you his girl?"

She flushed. "That's nothing to do with you!"

Weasel shrugged. Beside him, Stone's mud-caked face remained as inscrutable as ever.

Havoc came and leaned against Pirra, then hunkered down with her forepaws tucked beneath her. Poor Havoc. She hadn't tucked up her paws like that since she was a cub; and only then when she'd been really unhappy.

Pirra buried her nose in the lioness' deep, coarse fur. "I know," she whispered. "I miss him too." Havoc gave her a rasping lick. Then she twisted one ear, and a moment later, Pirra saw Echo silently alighting on a branch.

"Come down and have a bath," Pirra called to the falcon, stirring the shallows with her hand. "Lovely clean water, just how you like it!"

To her astonishment, the falcon only blinked.

But Echo *adored* bathing. Uneasily, Pirra noticed how utterly still the falcon was sitting. Normally she'd be preening, or sharpening her beak, or stretching her wings upward and over her back till they touched, then shaking them out with a crisp rustle, while looking about her with those great black eyes: always eager for new prey and new things.

Now she sat hunched, dull-eyed, and indifferent. Was this about missing Hylas, or was something else wrong?

At that moment, Pirra spotted an ear of ryegrass moving over the ground by her foot, apparently by itself. It was being carried on the back of the biggest ant she'd ever seen. The ant was the size of her fingernail and black; and now she saw a whole column of them, each bearing an ear of ryegrass and heading with grim determination toward a hole in the ground near where she knelt. The nest was seething with ants. Oh no, she thought.

Echo had spotted them too. The falcon's shrieks were ear-splitting—even the Marsh Dweller boys jumped. Havoc twitched her tail and watched Echo circling overhead, *kek-kekk*ing with terror.

Pirra heaved a sigh and got to her feet. "I'm sorry," she

told her guides, "but the one thing Echo's terrified of is ants. We'll have to move a bit farther uphill, or we'll never get any peace."

—⁙—

Weasel and Stone were building a shelter under an olive tree farther up the slope, and Pirra had woken a fire and plucked the two rock partridges she'd downed earlier with her slingshot. After leaving the guts in a bush as an offering to the Goddess, she'd skewered the birds on sticks and set them to roast.

Echo sat in the olive tree, swiveling her head as she scrutinized her new perch for ants. Pirra wondered what was wrong with the falcon. Normally, she gave her perch a quick check, and that was it.

"Here you are, Echo," she said, holding up a bloody scrap of partridge breast that she'd saved from the fire.

After an unusual amount of coaxing, Echo lit down onto Pirra's leather cuff, and stared at the meat. Then she seized it in her beak, flung it in the dust, and flew back to her perch.

Pirra noticed with alarm that despite the heat of the afternoon, the falcon had fluffed up her feathers to keep warm, and that instead of roosting on one leg as she always did, she was clutching her perch with both feet. She was panting too; as if flying even that short distance had exhausted her.

"Echo, what's *wrong*?"

Weasel glanced at the falcon over his shoulder. "Marsh fever," he muttered.

"What?" cried Pirra. "You mean she's *sick*?"

He nodded.

Stone approached, holding out something in his hand: a small lump of blackish powder.

"What's that?" Pirra said suspiciously.

Mutely, Stone shoved it in her face. Weasel answered for him. "Medicine. For the bird."

Pirra was surprised. "Thanks," she said.

Stone scowled, waiting for her to take the pellet.

After dusting off the meat that Echo had discarded, Pirra slit it and stuffed a little of the medicine inside. Then she coaxed the falcon back down again, and—after much persuasion—she got Echo to swallow a tiny shred of meat coated in the powder.

"We need to go uphill," said Weasel, startling her. "We need to show you the way to Dentra."

"What, now?" she snapped. "It'll be dark soon, and Echo—"

"Now."

She blew out a long breath.

"That trail there," said Weasel when they'd crested the hill above camp.

"Where?" panted Pirra. After several uncommunicative replies, she gathered that Dentra could be reached by following this stream to its source. The shrine itself was just below an arrow-shaped peak, itself overshadowed by the highest mountain of all—which Pirra could now see glaring down at her in the setting Sun: Mount Lykas.

That's where Hylas grew up, she thought. She wondered where he was and what he was doing. What if some peasant had spotted his fair hair and betrayed him to the Crows? What if he'd had a vision and collapsed, and there was no one to look after him?

The Marsh Dwellers had wandered off, and she returned to camp alone. They weren't there either, and neither was Havoc. Maybe at last she'd gone off to hunt.

Echo hadn't moved from her perch, and she was blinking and shivering. It seemed that the Marsh Dwellers' medicine didn't work on falcons.

The Dark came, and still the falcon kept checking her perch for ants.

Normally, a glance was enough before she settled to roost, but not now; and it was frightening to know that if she did spot an ant and had to fly off, she would tire after a few wingbeats, and have to alight in some other, perhaps even more ant-infested tree.

Why was she so frightened and so weak? Why were her eyes all scratchy? Why did she keep sneezing? She *hated* this, it was the worst thing that had ever happened to her. It was so humiliating, so un-falcon-like, having to clutch her perch with both feet and cower like a *pigeon*.

The she-lion hadn't seen any of this, as she'd gone hunting when the Dark had come; but the falcon would have felt a lot safer if she'd stayed—and that was even more humiliating. No falcon *needs* a lion. No falcon *needs* anyone.

A falcon merely chooses to be with another creature for a while, but she's always free to fly off whenever she likes.

The Dark wore on. The smelly little mud-people had left, and below her, the girl sat staring into the fire, missing the boy. The falcon missed him too. She hated that they'd all split up. They ought to have stayed together.

A shadow blotted out the stars, and the falcon cringed. The shadow passed. It was only a cloud, not the terrible spirits she'd sensed a few Lights ago.

Those terrible spirits were another thing to be afraid of in this awful place. They moved so fast, and They came without warning. If They came now, the falcon would be too weak to escape.

Below her, the girl was muttering in her deep, slow human speech. Now she was taking a burning stick from the fire and rising to her feet, and moving to the edge of the light.

Fearfully, the falcon shifted from foot to foot. Why couldn't the girl stay here and be safe?

Echo seemed ashamed of her weakness, and had refused to come down. She didn't understand that she was sick, and Pirra didn't know how to comfort her.

Pirra wasn't hungry, but she'd made herself eat half a rock partridge, and saved the rest for Weasel and Stone. They hadn't appeared, and now she'd realized that they weren't going to. That was why Weasel had insisted on showing her the way to Dentra: because he and Stone had left her and gone back to the marshes. From now on, she was on her own.

And her waterskin was empty. This made her annoyed with herself; she ought to have refilled it before it got dark. It also emphasized the fact that she was still learning how to survive in the wild—unlike Hylas, who'd been doing it all his life.

Muttering, she took a burning stick from the fire and shouldered the waterskin.

It was very dark beyond the firelight, and the forest was full of noises: shrieks, rustlings, the distant howls of wolves. From the sound of it, the wolves were far away in the mountains—but that was where she'd be heading at daybreak: deeper into this harsh, forbidding land, where Hylas felt at home, and she did not.

She thought of the huge, almost man-like prints she'd found yesterday, and which Weasel had said were bear. She'd never seen a bear. And today she'd spotted a gigantic boar snuffling around in the undergrowth. His tusks had been longer than her knife, and he'd cast her an irritable glance as he rooted for acorns.

All these wild creatures . . . And she couldn't rely on Havoc and Echo to warn her of danger, because Havoc was off hunting, and Echo was sick.

"Come on, Pirra," she said out loud. "No point feeling sorry for yourself!"

The pool glinted in the fitful moonlight, and the pine-scented air rang with the song of night crickets. A fish plopped. The waterskin gurgled as Pirra held it under.

She spotted movement on the other side of the pool, and broke into a smile. Two great moon-silvered eyes were gazing at her from among the reeds.

"There you are, Havoc!" she called softly. "I'm so glad you're back! Did you have a successful hunt?"

Like all lions, Havoc appeared gray by night, and had an uncanny ability to melt into her surroundings: Pirra could hardly make her out. But instead of splashing across the pool and giving her a boisterous greeting, the lioness kept her head low between her shoulder blades, as if she was play-hunting.

Pirra yawned. "Sorry, Havoc, but I'm far too tired to play."

The night wind stirred the reeds, but Havoc went on staring.

Pirra's belly turned over. There was nothing playful about those eyes. They were colder than any she'd ever seen.

And this wasn't play-stalking, this was in deadly earnest.

Because this lion wasn't Havoc.

The two warriors on the riverbank looked dusty and fed up: They were a long way from camp, and Lord Telamon would not be pleased that they hadn't found Hylas' trail. One was swatting midges and glaring at the noonday Sun, while the other used his helmet to douse himself with water.

"Over here!" shouted their comrades farther downriver.

"At *last*," grumbled the one with the helmet, and the pair moved off to join their companions, pushing through the giant fennel on the bank—and quite unaware of Hylas, hiding on the other side.

Their voices drifted toward him. "It's the Outsider's tracks, all right."

"By the look of them, heading downstream."

Yes, you go on thinking that, Hylas told them silently. When it came to tracking, Crows were no match for an Outsider; they hadn't spotted that he'd set a false trail.

He waited till they were long gone, then started *up*stream. The important thing now was to shake the

Crows off his trail. Once he was rid of them for sure, he would think about the dagger.

After climbing for a bit, he came to a rocky stretch where the river went crashing and foaming over rapids. Tamarisk and walnut trees gave good cover, but beneath them it was hot and airless, and swarming with midges.

Hylas felt battered after his fight with Telamon, and the cut on his forearm throbbed. His head was throbbing too, although he couldn't remember bumping it on his way down the gully, and despite the heat of the Sun, he felt slightly shivery.

He was also angry with himself. He'd had Telamon at his mercy, on his knees and half stunned. If it had been the other way around, Telamon would have killed him without hesitation.

So why couldn't I kill him? thought Hylas. Because I've never killed anyone? Or because he was once my best friend?

Or was I *scared*? Is that what stopped me? Am I a coward, like my father?

Above the rapids, he came to a green meadow, noisy with crickets and spiked with purple thistles as tall as men. Thick woods hid the river, echoing with birdsong.

Hylas had no idea where he was. All he knew was that the mountains rearing above him marked the border between Messenia and Lykonia—and that the highest mountain of all, Mount Lykas, was somewhere to the east—although out of sight. He'd grown up on Mount Lykas. He knew every goat trail, every ravine and secret pass, every lightning-blasted tree. If he could climb high enough, maybe he could see it; then he'd know where he was.

Of course, Telamon might guess that this was exactly what he would do, but that was a risk he'd have to take.

He had his knife, slingshot, waterskin, and the Marsh Dwellers' bag of provisions. Sitting under a tree, he ate a chunk of dried eel and half a reed-pollen cake. The eel was rancid, the cake gritty and dry; he had to wash them down with a drink—although, as the waterskin was made of trout hide, that tasted fishy too.

The Marsh Dwellers had also given him medicines: a little wovengrass pouch containing a slimy yellow salve, and a smaller one full of black powder.

"The salve is for your jellyfish stings," they'd said. "The powder is poppy-seed tea, good for marsh fever; but you need to take it as soon as you feel it coming on."

Like everything else, the salve smelled fishy, but it had helped with his jellyfish blisters, so Hylas smeared some on his grazes and on the cut on his arm, and it eased the pain a bit.

When he got to his feet, his blood soughed in his ears and his head throbbed; but it wasn't the ache he got before a vision, it felt like too much Sun, so he ignored it and started upriver.

He nearly walked straight past the hoofprints in the mud.

They were bigger than a donkey's, and had clearly been

made by a horse: a horse who'd stopped to drink, spreading its forelegs wide to reach the water, as horses do. After that it had cropped some fennel, then headed upstream, as Hylas was doing now. As it went, it had dragged its tether behind it: At one point in its trail, Hylas spotted faint drag-marks.

He found Jinx around the next bend in the river. The rope attached to his bridle had snagged in a thorn bush, and the stallion was making it worse by attacking the bush. He kept lunging at it, then sidling around and lunging again. He seemed not to have realized that by going in a circle around it, he was shortening the tether and thus restricting himself even more.

Hylas waited till the tether was wound so short that Jinx was well and truly stuck; then he stepped slowly into the open.

"Steady there, Jinx," he said quietly, so that the horse wouldn't think he was sneaking up.

Jinx flattened his ears and tried to rear—but the tether held him fast.

"Steady," repeated Hylas, approaching the horse from the other side of the thorn bush and holding up his hands, so that Jinx could see that he wasn't holding a stick.

After tugging so long at his tether, the stallion's mouth was raw and bleeding. His flanks bore scars from old beatings, as well as fresh, oozing weals: It seemed that despite the horse's value, Telamon hadn't spared the whip. No wonder Jinx hated and feared all men.

"Steady, Jinx." Hylas put out his hand to let the horse catch his scent.

Jinx showed the whites of his eyes, flattening his ears and flaring his large round nostrils.

"Remember me? I rode you once, two summers ago." As he talked, Hylas started disentangling the rope, careful not to look Jinx in the eye or get too close, which would make him feel trapped. "I gave you food, remember? You stomped on the cheese, but you ate the olives. Then you ran away."

Again, Hylas extended his hand. Jinx tensed. Hylas waited. Then he laid his palm very lightly on the horse's shoulder. Jinx shuddered and snorted, shifting from foot to foot. "That's good," murmured Hylas, gently stroking the hot, sweaty muscles. "You know I won't hurt you, don't you, Jinx?"

Again the stallion's nostrils flared; but he was listening. Hylas thought he might be getting somewhere.

All at once, Jinx jerked up his head and set his ears right back, rolling his eyes and snorting with alarm. The next instant, Hylas heard it too: men's voices, somewhere downriver. The Crows were better at tracking than he'd thought: It hadn't taken them long to find the right trail.

"Sorry, Jinx," muttered Hylas, "but I've got to get out of here fast!" Wrenching the tether free of the thorns, he scrambled onto the stallion's back, grabbed a handful of mane, and dug in his heels.

Jinx hated the Crows as much as Hylas did, and after his first outraged squeal at having a man on his back, he shot off across the meadow. Hylas clung on, bending low against the horse's straining neck, and praying that he could manage to stay on.

Shouts behind him, and an arrow hissed past his thigh. Another thudded into the grass by Jinx's foreleg.

Galloping around a spur, they plunged into a thicket of willows. Branches whipped Hylas' limbs. He clung on grimly. If he fell off now, he was finished.

Now they were bursting out of the willows and lurching up a hillside thick with bracken and pines, then skittering down a steep, densely wooded slope. At the bottom, a fallen sapling blocked the way. Hylas tugged on the tether to guide Jinx around it, but the rope was only attached to one side of the bridle and the stallion ignored him, leaping over the sapling and coming down with a thud that nearly threw Hylas off his back.

On and on they went, up hills and gullies, around spurs, while the shouts of the Crows faded behind them. Hylas' arms and legs were screaming for rest; he couldn't stay on much longer. Jinx was also tiring. And he seemed to have decided that he'd had enough of this infuriating human, for suddenly he swerved and made straight for a low-hanging branch, to scrape Hylas off.

He'd tried that trick two summers ago, and Hylas ducked just in time.

Jinx tried another trick, jolting to a sudden halt, to pitch

Hylas over his neck. Again Hylas was ready, and managed to cling on.

Finally, Jinx seemed to realize that the simplest way was the best: He put down his head and bucked.

Hylas went flying, and landed in a juniper bush.

IO

Painfully, Hylas got to his feet and started plodding up the valley. No broken bones, but lots of bruises and an aching head.

Jinx was long gone. The immediate threat of the Crows was gone too, but Hylas was still lost. He decided his best chance was to keep climbing, in the hopes that he could get a glimpse of Mount Lykas.

And after that, what?

He knew now that the dagger was at Lapithos, the Crows' ancestral stronghold on the lower slopes of Mount Lykas, which had once been Telamon's home, and had been taken over by Koronos. But Lapithos was said to be impregnable, with walls ten cubits thick—and with Koronos and the dagger inside, it would be bristling with guards. Even if he found his way there, he couldn't steal the dagger on his own.

Maybe he should try to find what remained of the rebels, and see if he could persuade them to help?

Pondering this, he rounded a spur.

It turned out that Jinx hadn't gone far after all. He'd found himself a shady spot in a ravine, and was quietly cropping the grass.

Catching Hylas' scent, the stallion jerked up his head and stared at him.

Hylas wondered what to do. The ravine was steep-sided and narrow, and behind Jinx, it had been blocked by a rockfall; it should be possible to trap the stallion by closing off this end with dead wood. But getting Jinx to trust him would take time, and it might prove impossible—not to mention dangerous: Those hooves could split his skull like an eggshell.

And yet. He could cover more ground and find the rebels faster on horseback—as well as escape the Crows.

There was something else too. If he left Jinx now, then sooner or later, the stallion would be recaptured. More whips, more beatings. Jinx needed Hylas as much as Hylas needed Jinx.

Hylas also had a strange feeling that if he helped Jinx, then the Lady of the Wild Things might help Issi. He'd felt something like this before, when he'd first found Havoc on Thalakrea: a small, frightened lion cub in danger of starving to death. Jinx was neither small nor starving; but the feeling was the same.

Slowly, with no sudden moves, Hylas picked up one end of a fallen sapling, and dragged it across the mouth of the ravine.

"The hardest thing about taming a horse," a fellow slave called Zan had once told Hylas, "is taming your own feelings. If *you're* scared, the horse will know it in a heartbeat, and he'll use it against you."

Hylas clearly wasn't doing a very good job of concealing his alarm, because as he tried for the tenth time to approach Jinx, the stallion tossed his head and stamped one hoof, flaring those nostrils as big as plums; then he lunged at Hylas, baring his yellow teeth.

For the tenth time, Hylas raised his long bendy stick, to the end of which he'd tied a scrap of his tunic: not to strike, merely to block the horse's attack.

Jinx shied away from the rag, snorting and sidestepping. Foam flecked his chestnut flanks: He was trembling with anger and fear. Mostly fear. He knew he was trapped, and he hated the smell of the human who'd done this. He hated all humans.

Hylas lowered the stick and waited. The Sun beat down on his head, and he longed to cool off in the little brook he heard chattering among the rocks.

At last, Jinx quieted a little. Talking softly, Hylas took one small step toward him. Jinx eyed the rag and prepared to attack again.

Zan had told Hylas about the trick with the stick when they'd been slaves in the Thalakrean mines. Zan's father had been a horse-tamer, and Zan had enjoyed talking of him; he used to say proudly that Arzawans were the best horse-tamers in the world.

"The main thing is patience," he'd told Hylas. "Let the horse come to you, when he's ready."

Which would be fine, if you had days and days to spare . . .

The Sun was getting low when Jinx suddenly seemed to lose interest in attacking Hylas, and threw down his head and snatched a few mouthfuls of grass.

This time, Hylas got close enough to touch the horse's shoulder with the rag: a gentle caress that made Jinx's withers twitch—although he didn't move away.

Slowly, Hylas passed the rag over the gleaming chestnut back and down the stallion's rump. He lowered the stick. He took another step forward. He held out his hand.

Jinx put back his ears and made a halfhearted attempt to bite, which Hylas blocked with the stick.

The next time he tried, Jinx didn't bite. He stood tensely, but he let Hylas lay his palm on his shoulder.

Hylas felt the heat coming off the stallion, and breathed his rich horsey scent. Jinx ground his teeth and shook his head irritably, as if the bridle hurt, and Hylas noticed that his mouth was crusted with scabs. Now he saw why. Fastened between both sides of the bridle and forced between the stallion's teeth was a jagged bronze bar: That must hurt with every yank of the rope.

Hylas had never seen such a thing, but he remembered something Zan had told him. "It's called a bit," the

Arzawan boy had said, his voice dripping with scorn. "We *never* use them, we don't need to! Only bad horsemen use bits, to hide their lack of skill."

"Let's get this off you, shall we?" murmured Hylas. Still talking under his breath, he shielded Jinx's eyes with one hand and slipped the bridle over his head with the other, then gently eased the bit from between Jinx's teeth.

Jinx looked startled, as if he couldn't believe what had just happened. He watched as Hylas slung the bridle over his arm and walked over to the brook.

With his knife, Hylas cut off the hated bit, stowing it in his pouch in case it came in useful; then he washed the bridle and scrubbed it with grit, to take away the smell of the Crows. Finally, he rubbed his palms all over it, working his own scent into the leather, then hung it on a branch, so that Jinx could get used to it and sniff it whenever he liked.

After that, things improved faster than Hylas had dared hope. When he wandered off to look for herbs, Jinx watched him go; and when he returned to the brook, the stallion ambled closer, then started cropping the grass. By nightfall, he let Hylas smear a poultice of mud and mashed wormwood leaves on the weals on his flanks; and the Marsh Dwellers' yellow salve proved an unexpected success when Hylas patted it gently on the scabs around the horse's mouth, as Jinx seemed to like the taste.

He liked it too when Hylas scratched his neck with his fingers. And he *loved* it when Hylas started unplaiting his mane, which the Crows had braided cruelly tight. Jinx stood patiently, swishing his tail at the flies, and when Hylas had finished, the stallion gave a luxurious shudder from nose to tail, then threw himself down and rolled in the grass, kicking his hooves in the air and snorting with delight.

By now, there was just enough light left for Hylas to make a rough shelter of branches. The Crows would still be far away; he would head off in the morning.

He was exhausted, but he slept badly, as his head was aching even worse than before; but whenever he woke, he was comforted by the sounds of Jinx's soft slow breathing outside, and the occasional swish of his tail.

The next morning, Hylas smeared the last of the Marsh Dwellers' salve on the bridle, and held it out for Jinx to sniff. When the horse didn't shy, Hylas slipped the bridle over his head.

Jinx contented himself with a little sidestepping, but when Hylas walked a few paces, he allowed himself to be led. And some time later, he let Hylas ease himself gently onto his back.

The next night was colder, as they'd climbed higher into the foothills.

Hylas camped among pines at the edge of a steep forested gorge that echoed with birdsong. He'd seen no trace of the Crows all day, but he didn't dare risk a fire. Jinx stood nearby, dozing with his head down.

Hylas now had a rough idea where he was, because just before sunset, he'd glimpsed Mount Lykas in the distance. It was to the southeast, but closer than he'd thought. He'd never seen it from this angle, and as its triple fangs glared red in the last of the light, it looked both familiar and oddly alien. He'd had a hard life on that mountain, but Issi had been with him. As he watched the light dying on its peaks, he was gripped by both pain and longing.

Huddled in his shelter, he tried to force down a scrap of dried eel, but he wasn't hungry. His head was throbbing, and he kept shivering.

He wished he had more of a lead on the rebels. During the day, he'd come upon a few tracks that might have been theirs, as well as a false trail that would have fooled anyone except an Outsider. This told him that the rebels knew these foothills well, and that it probably wouldn't be a case of him finding them, but of *them* finding *him*. He was beginning to wish they would.

But who *were* they, these rebels about whom he'd heard only rumors? The Marsh Dwellers said they were peasants, fishermen, and ex-slaves. Hylas wondered if Periphas was among them; he was an ex-slave, and a Messenian. Hylas had met him in the Thalakrean mines. Together they'd survived a cave-in, and escaped the island when it blew up, then wandered the Sea with other ex-slaves, seeking the way back to Akea. Periphas hated the Crows as much as Hylas did: If he'd found his way to his homeland, he would have joined the rebels for sure.

And what about Akastos, was he with them too? Hylas

admired Akastos above all other men; for a while, he'd even hoped that he would turn out to be his father. But he'd last seen Akastos in the spring, on Keftiu, and even if he had returned to Akea, he'd probably be far in the north near Mycenae, fighting for his farm that the Crows had taken from him.

Although even that was unlikely, because Akastos was on the run from the Angry Ones. Why would he return to Akea, with Them haunting the skies? Years ago, Akastos had been tricked by the lies of the Crows into fighting and killing his own brother. Ever since, he'd been on the run: both from the Crows, and from the spirits of vengeance . . .

The thought of the Angry Ones made Hylas shiver. Under his breath, he muttered the ancient charm against Them. He went on shivering. He couldn't stop.

If Havoc had been with him, she would have slumped against him to warm him up with her great, furry bulk, and Pirra would have made him some herb tea—or more likely rolled her eyes and told him with a grin to do it himself. He missed them savagely. And his headache was much worse. Fuzzily, he wondered if he was sick.

Somewhere close by, a nightingale sang. Again, he thought of Pirra. She'd heard one for the first time when they'd camped in the Keftian hills last spring. It had been midnight, and in the stillness, the bird's loud song had woken her up.

"What's *that*?" she'd muttered crossly. "What kind of idiot bird sings in the middle of the night?"

Hylas had laughed. "A nightingale, of course."

"Huh! Well, I wish it'd shut up and let me sleep!"

Then she'd seen the funny side of it, and burst out laughing, and together they'd chucked stones at the bushes until the nightingale flew off to wake up someone else . . .

Jinx nosed Hylas' shoulder, and he jolted awake. His head felt as if metal bands were tightening around it, and he was freezing, yet drenched in sweat. Suddenly, his thoughts flew to the Marsh Dwellers' platform among the reeds. He remembered the sick people huddled on their mats. Marsh fever. He had marsh fever.

And it was getting worse fast. Waves of sickness were surging through him, and he felt as if he was going to throw up.

Remembering the little pouch of poppy-seed tea, he rummaged in the bag. He couldn't find it; it must have fallen out.

The last time he'd felt this ill was in Egypt, when he'd been stung by a scorpion—but then Pirra had been with him. He'd clung to her hand, gripping so hard that she'd had bruises for days.

His teeth were chattering uncontrollably, shivers shaking him from top to toe. Crows or no Crows, he had to make a fire.

He dropped his strike-fire and couldn't find it in the dark. Instead he scrabbled around for sticks to rub together. It was all he could do to pick up a couple, but he was so weak he'd never manage it. He *had* to get warm, or he would die. But if he couldn't wake a fire . . .

Once, when Issi was six, she'd caught a chill from swimming for too long in a lake, and Hylas had tried a cure he'd seen the peasants use. He'd found a donkey dozing in a barley patch, and laid Issi on its back, with her arms and legs hanging down on either side and her belly against the beast's warm, furry back. She'd lain like that all night, and by morning, the warmth of the donkey's body had done its work, and she was better.

Jinx gave Hylas a doubtful glance when he lurched toward him. Then the stallion seemed to sense that something was wrong, and after a bit of sidestepping, he allowed Hylas to struggle onto his back.

Hylas lay with his cheek against the horse's neck, and felt Jinx's blissful warmth stealing through his body. Jinx shifted his weight from hoof to hoof, and he nearly slid off. He mumbled a prayer to the Lady of the Wild Things to keep the stallion still, because if he did fall off, he'd never have the strength to climb back on.

Jinx's neck drooped as he began to doze. Hylas' thoughts became tangled and confused. He was no longer in camp but on a shoulder of Mount Lykas, and Issi was standing under a pine tree. Her arms were crossed on her scrawny chest, and she was scowling at him.

"Why did you never come and *find* me?" she demanded indignantly. "I waited and waited, but you never *came!*"

He wanted to tell her that he'd tried, but that all sorts

of things had gotten in the way: Thalakrea, Keftiu, Egypt . . . Above all, the Crows.

"And now I have to find the dagger," he tried to tell her, "or we'll never be free of them." But he couldn't move his lips, and no sound came.

Then Issi was gone, and Havoc was licking his foot with her hot, rasping tongue—and here was Pirra, walking past him with her ax over her shoulder.

"Pirra!" Hylas tried to call, but all he managed was a raspy wheeze.

Pirra turned her head, and her dark eyes looked straight through him as she whistled to Havoc.

He called again, but the dream faded and they were gone.

There were lions in these mountains; the she-lion could hear them. *This is my land! Mine!* roared an unknown female.

That female was too far off to be dangerous, but there was another lion that smelled much nearer. Earlier, the she-lion had come upon the remains of a kill, picked clean by vultures. She'd passed bushes that had been scent-marked only a few Lights ago; and just now, as she was plodding through the Dark, she'd paused at a tree to do some scratching, and when she'd risen on her hind legs, she'd found that its bark was already claw-marked: Another lion had gotten there before her.

She'd smelled that he was barely full-grown, and not very sure of himself; but his claw-marks were higher than hers, which told her that he was bigger.

The she-lion was too miserable to care. With every Light and Dark, she missed the boy more. She missed his foresty scent and his yowling calls when he wanted her to come. She missed their games with the ball of sticks, when he would throw it and she would race after it, batting it between her forepaws while he tried to get it back.

She even missed him telling her off. Like that time when she'd taken his head affectionately in her jaws, and he'd given a muffled shout and punched her in the chest. She'd hardly felt the punch, it was like being tickled by a moth, but the boy had seemed to think he'd overdone it; he'd kept saying sorry. She'd found that very funny.

In all the time they'd been together, they'd never had a *real* fight. So *why* had he sent her away? Why didn't he want her anymore?

Since he'd left, everything was chewed up and wrong. The girl was miserable. The two muddy little humans had left just when the she-lion was getting to like them, especially the younger one, who used to stroke the she-lion when the girl wasn't around. There'd been something odd about that little human; something the she-lion couldn't put her paw on, but which had made her curious.

And now there was something badly amiss with the falcon. She was too weak to hunt, and she sat shivering on her branch. The she-lion sensed that the girl was really worried about her.

The she-lion was worried too, which was actually quite surprising, because at times the falcon could be extremely scornful, and looked down on the she-lion because she couldn't fly. But the falcon did have her uses. She was good at picking ticks out of the she-lion's fur in hard-to-reach places, and she hated the crow-humans as much as the she-lion did, and was brilliant at spotting them from very far away.

If only she would get better. If only the boy would come back, and the pride could be together. These were good mountains, with plenty of prey and only a few humans. They could find somewhere without lions, and stay here forever, instead of always moving on . . .

The wind growled at the pine trees, and in the bracken, a boar jerked up his head at the she-lion's scent. Ignoring him, she leaped onto a rock to snuff the smells.

That was when she heard the falcon's *ek-ek-ek* alarm calls. The she-lion's pelt tightened. Something told her this wasn't about ants.

The next moment, she heard the girl shouting. She sounded frightened and fierce. The she-lion leaped off the rock and sped through the forest.

As she drew near the lair, she caught a new smell on the wind: *lion*. She smelled that he was male, full-grown and big. It was the same lion who'd claw-marked that tree.

The falcon was in her tree, shrieking with alarm. The girl was on one side of the wet, the male lion on the other. The girl was clutching a stick that glimmered faintly, while in the other forepaw she gripped her big shiny claw. But against that lion, it would be as much use as a twig.

The she-lion took in the male's heavy mane and his massive shoulders. He didn't sense her: She'd made sure that she was downwind, and he was intent on his prey.

Noiselessly, the male retreated into the reeds, so that the girl couldn't see him. He began sidling around the edge of the wet. The girl cast about her, trying to spot him; but like all humans, she was nearly blind in the Dark, and she couldn't smell at all. She was looking the wrong way.

The she-lion dropped to her belly and lowered her tail, so that the male wouldn't spot her tail tuft.

The girl was still looking the wrong way, oblivious of the male lion belly-crawling closer. He was preparing to leap from behind and snap her spine with one shake of his jaws. And still he didn't smell the she-lion stalking *him*.

She slunk nearer, placing each paw with silent stealth. She saw his haunches bunch as he got ready to spring. She *charged*.

She landed on his back and sank her claws into his flanks. With a startled roar he whipped around and bit her shoulder. Snarling and raking his muzzle with her claws, she wrenched herself free. She was aware of the falcon shrieking, the girl yowling and waving her burning stick; then the male was on her again and they were locked together, a snarling, snapping frenzy of teeth and claws. The male was stronger but she was faster, and she was fighting for her pride. She dodged most of his paw-swipes; he couldn't escape hers.

At last they sprang apart, panting and gnashing their fangs. The she-lion's shoulder was on fire, but the male had come off worse: His muzzle was pouring blood, and she'd bitten off his ear. She *roared* at him. He roared back.

But she knew the fight had gone out of him, and he turned tail and fled.

She bounded a few paces after him, then roared again. *This is my pride! Mine!* she roared. *Don't come back!*

The falcon stopped shrieking and folded her wings; she looked utterly spent. The girl sheathed her great claw and rushed to the she-lion, patting her with her little furless paws and talking fervently in human talk. Then she fetched some wet and poured it over the gash on the she-lion's shoulder—even though it was nothing a good lick wouldn't sort out.

Together, they padded back to the fire, where the girl gave the she-lion meat: a partridge, very burned, but with the feathers taken off, which helped. On her branch, the falcon peered down at them and sneezed. The girl fed the fire more sticks, and sat watching the she-lion crunching up the bird.

When the she-lion had finished, she stretched out beside the girl and started licking the gash on her shoulder clean. She smelled that the male lion was already far away. Good. She didn't think he would return.

Better even than that, she finally understood why the boy had sent her away. She hadn't done anything wrong, and he wasn't angry with her. He wanted her to protect the girl and the falcon. He wanted her to look after the pride until he came back.

This made the she-lion feel extremely proud and much, *much* better.

12

Hylas woke with Jinx's bony withers digging into his chest. His head no longer hurt and he felt much better: The marsh fever was gone.

He lay with his eyes shut, enjoying the warmth of the stallion's big solid body, and listening to the birds waking up in the gorge.

Waking up . . . he thought muzzily. Must be dawn. In a while, I'll slide off and find something to eat . . . but not yet.

Some time later, he woke again. Jinx was snorting and sidestepping. "What is it now?" mumbled Hylas. He felt weak and disinclined to move. Without bothering to open his eyes, he slithered off the horse's back. His knees gave way and he sank to the ground.

Someone sniggered. Hands grabbed his shoulders and yanked him upright, and a deep voice said, "Now what have we here?"

"What if he's telling the truth and he really is the Outsider the Crows are after?" said the first rebel, an enormous man with a tangled black beard, short bowed legs, and a massive greenstone ax slung over one shoulder.

His companion snorted a laugh. "What, you want to hand him over and get the reward?"

"Course not! But if he *is* the one, the Crows might be hot on his heels!"

"I thought of that too," said the other. He was thin and wiry, and his pinched features weren't improved by a straggly red beard. Like his companion, his "armor" was a grimy tunic of quilted homespun and a thick leather cap. His weapons were those of a peasant: a granite hammer thrust in his belt, a flint sickle, and a flint-tipped spear that he was pointing at Hylas' chest.

"You *say* you're an Outsider," he said suspiciously, "and you do sort of look like one. But what's an Outsider doing with a horse and a fine bronze knife? No Outsider I ever seen had a knife like that! Where'd you get it, eh?"

"Egypt," said Hylas.

"Where's that, then?" snorted the big man with the black beard.

"Never heard of it!" spat the thin man with the red beard.

Hylas made no reply. His plan to allow the rebels to find him had been accomplished with alarming ease. What he hadn't anticipated was that they'd think he was a Crow spy. And they didn't seem the kind who bothered about taking prisoners.

Behind them, Jinx was tugging in vain at his tether, but the big man had tied him firmly to a tree, and he couldn't break free.

They'd tied Hylas up too, pinioning his arms and making him stand on the edge of the gorge, with his back to the drop. It was all he could do to stay on his feet, swaying and squinting in the Sun.

"I still think he's the one," insisted Blackbeard. "Yellow hair, Crow tattoo—"

"It's Mountain Clan," said Hylas. "Not Crow."

"That's no better," snapped Redbeard. "When the Crows attacked Mycenae all them years ago, the Mountain Outsiders wouldn't fight!" He jabbed his spear at Hylas. "If you're Mountain Clan, you're a coward!"

Slowly, Hylas shook his head. "I'm Mountain Clan, but I'm no coward."

"Where'd you get the horse?" demanded Blackbeard.

"Found him," said Hylas. "He escaped from the Crows. So did I."

"What were you doing with the Crows?" said Redbeard.

Hylas hesitated. "I'll tell your leader."

"No, you'll tell us, or we'll chuck you off the cliff."

"All right," said Hylas. "I'm after the dagger of Koronos. I found out from the Crows that it's at Lapithos. I *let* you find me because I want you to help me steal it."

There was an astonished silence. Then both men burst out laughing. Blackbeard leaned on his ax and roared till the tears ran down his cheeks. Redbeard collapsed against a tree, wheezing through a mouthful of broken teeth.

"Oh, that's a good one, that is!" he panted. "Now tell us the truth, eh? And I meant it about chucking you off the cliff."

"I meant it about the dagger," said Hylas.

"Listen, boy," said Blackbeard, wiping his eyes. "Maybe you was once a goatherd on Mount Lykas, like you said. And maybe you did lose your sister when the Crows attacked your camp. But we don't *know* if that's true, do we, 'cos we never *been* to Lykonia! All we *know* is you come out of nowhere wearing a Crow tattoo, with a fine Crow horse, and spouting some daft plan for getting us all killed!"

"He's got to be a spy," said Redbeard.

"But if I'm not," retorted Hylas, "and if you chuck me off this cliff, you'll be in deep trouble with your leader!" He was bluffing; he had no idea who their leader was. But they didn't know that.

Blackbeard blew his nose in his hand and wiped it down his thigh. "You *say* you want to join us. How do we know you're not a Crow spy? Name one rebel from round here. Go on, just one."

Hylas thought of Akastos. But Akastos had made him swear never to reveal his name to a living soul; besides, he was from Mycenae, far to the north. "Periphas," he said uncertainly.

The men exchanged glances.

"What's he look like?" said Redbeard.

"Um—about my height," said Hylas. "Brown hair and eyes, broken nose—"

"How'd it get broke?"

"He stepped on a hoe when he was fifteen and it bashed

him in the face. He was too embarrassed to tell his friends, so he said he broke it in a fight."

Blackbeard laughed. "Well, I never knew that!"

"Do you know him?" Hylas cried eagerly.

"How come you didn't mention him before?" said Redbeard.

"I didn't know that you knew him! We were slaves together in the mines of Thalakrea; we escaped in the same ship! He—he's got a tattoo like mine on his forearm, the Crows did that to all the slaves, only I altered mine; that's why it's like the Mountain Clan's! Tell him I'm here! He'll vouch for me, I know he will!"

Another exchange of glances. Then Blackbeard shrugged. "Ah, where's the harm? If he's lying, we'll soon find out."

"What's your name, boy?" said Redbeard.

Again Hylas hesitated. "Just tell him it's Flea."

It was night when Hylas' blindfold was finally removed. Blackbeard—whose real name turned out to be Nomios—dragged him off Jinx's back. His belly hurt from the stallion's withers, and he was still a bit weak.

In the moonlight, he made out Mount Lykas, rearing high above. It was closer than before, and he knew at once where he was. The rebel camp was on a mountain to the northwest.

Among the trees, he saw pine-bough shelters and a large, motley throng of peasants, fishermen, and even a few warriors, huddled around fires. Many had bandaged limbs and heads; some were sewing each other's wounds or tending their own. Their faces were seamed with dirt, hardship, and fatigue, and they glanced stonily at Hylas.

There were women among them, no less dirty and grim, and children, and large shaggy mountain dogs who reminded him painfully of his own dog Scram, whom the Crows had killed. The camp was surprisingly well ordered. He saw sacks of barley, skins of oil, and bunches of rue and wormwood hung to dry in the smoke. From cauldrons set over the fires he caught the mouthwatering smell of barley gruel.

Ekion, whom he still thought of as Redbeard, hurried off to find Periphas. Nomios left Hylas in the charge of some peasants, and led Jinx to a clearing where a small herd of donkeys was grazing. Hylas watched anxiously, but the big man handled Jinx with brisk gentleness as he tied him to a pine with a long rope. Jinx flattened his ears and lunged at the nearest donkey, who gave a deafening bray and bit him on the shoulder. Jinx leaped back, startled. The donkey tossed its head and resumed grazing. Jinx shook himself, and did the same.

"Over here." Ekion jerked his head, and he and Nomios led Hylas through the trees. They came to a fire around which sat a group of tired-looking warriors. One of them was instantly familiar, and Hylas broke into a grin.

"Periphas!" he cried. "Oh, it's so good to see you again!"

"And you, Hylas," Periphas said gravely; but he didn't return the grin. His eyes were red-rimmed with exhaustion, and there was a bloodstained bandage around his shin. Like his companions, he wore battered armor of dusty brown rawhide over a tunic of grimy quilted linen. His hair had grown since Hylas had last seen him, and it was braided, like a warrior's.

He *is* a warrior, Hylas thought in surprise.

"So it's true," said Ekion, "he really does know you."

"He saved my life down the mines," said Periphas without taking his eyes off Hylas. "Later, he warned us that the mountain was going to blow up. That didn't only save me, it saved Glaukos and Medon and many others." Then to Hylas: "Last time I saw you was on Keftiu, you went off to look for your girl. Did you find her?"

"Yes," said Hylas. Why did this feel like an interrogation? Why wasn't Periphas glad to see him?

Ekion stepped forward and handed Periphas Hylas' knife and his *wedjat* eye amulet. "We found these on him."

Periphas took them in silence. Then he heaved a sigh and rubbed a hand over his face. "These are Egyptian," he said quietly.

"Yes," said Hylas. "But what's—"

"Oh, Hylas. I really hoped it wasn't true. But now I see that it is." He met Hylas' eyes, and his own were bright with anger. "It was you who gave the dagger of Koronos to the Crows."

The other warriors leaped to their feet and drew their swords. All the rebels within earshot crowded around, shouting angrily.

"He done that? He don't deserve to live!"

"String him up from the nearest tree!"

"I knew he was a wrong 'un the moment I saw him!"

"Enough!" cried Periphas—and silence fell. "Why, Hylas?" he said in a low voice. "Tell me why you did it."

Hylas lifted his chin. "Telamon had Pirra," he said levelly. "He would have killed her if I hadn't thrown him the dagger."

Periphas furrowed his brow. "Pirra . . . That's the girl you went to look for on Keftiu—yes?"

Hylas nodded.

"Oh, Hylas," Periphas said bitterly. "I hope she was worth it."

Hylas swallowed. "How did you know any of this?"

Again Periphas sighed. "One of the Crows on Telamon's ship deserted. He'd begun to have his doubts that he was on the right side when Telamon left his kinswoman to the crocodiles. Then he saw a lion and a falcon coming to your aid, and he thought if you had the favor of the gods, he'd be a fool to go against you; so when they got back to Akea, he jumped ship and joined us." He paused. "I didn't believe his story. I couldn't *bring* myself to think that you—*you*—would have given the dagger to the Crows."

Hylas licked his lips. "I did what I had to, Periphas— and I'd do it again. But killing me won't help you beat them." He paused. "I told you once about the Oracle: *If an Outsider wields the blade, the House of Koronos burns . . .*"

"And what good is that now?" burst out Periphas. "Because of you, they got the dagger back! Because of you, they can't be beaten, and we lost the battle in the north, and along with it half of Messenia, and good men died! All that might have been different if you hadn't thrown it to Telamon!"

To that, Hylas had no answer. "But now it's at Lapithos," he said. Briefly, he told Periphas of his encounter with Telamon. "I'd only guessed that it's there, but I knew from Telamon's face that my guess was right!"

"What if you did?" snapped Periphas. "You still don't know for sure."

"Periphas, I came to you," Hylas said urgently. "I *let* your men find me—because I need your help to go to Lapithos and get it back!"

Periphas stared at him in disbelief. Then he gave a mirthless laugh. "*What*?" he said with dangerous quietness. "Attack a stronghold with walls ten cubits thick? Look around you, Hylas! Half my men are wounded and the other half don't know how to fight!"

Rising to his feet, he took a few steps away—painfully because of his injured shin—then returned and loomed over Hylas. "Most of these men here aren't warriors like the Crows," he said between his teeth. "We're not an army, and we lost the battle in the north because we don't have a leader who could make us into one! And now—

now, at long last, the rightful High Chieftain of Mycenae has returned, when none of us ever dreamed that was possible—and maybe, just *maybe*, he could help us beat them, but he—" He broke off with a scowl, as if he'd said too much.

Hylas stared up at him. "But—I thought the true High Chieftain was dead! I thought the Crows killed him fifteen years ago, when they took over Mycenae!"

"So did we all," muttered Periphas. "But now he's back. Although it looks as if he's come too late."

"This isn't getting us anywhere," growled Ekion. "The boy gave the dagger to the Crows, that's all we need to know!"

"He's right," put in another man. "Let's kill him and have done with it—"

"Not till I say so," cut in Periphas.

"But—"

"I'm in charge here, Ekion. Hylas saved my life on Thalakrea. Whatever he's done, I won't be the one to order his death."

"So what do we do with him?" said Ekion.

Periphas put his hands on his hips. "We'll take him to the High Chieftain. Let him decide."

⸻

Once again Hylas was blindfolded, and this time he was flung over a donkey's back, even bonier and more uncomfortable than Jinx. The last he heard of the rebels' camp was the stallion's piercing neigh. Jinx didn't like being abandoned. Hylas hoped the rebels would care for him well.

Fortunately, they hadn't gone far before he was hauled off the donkey and led down a steep, stony slope into what he guessed from the echoes to be a cave. He smelled wine and woodsmoke. His blindfold was wrenched off.

Blinking in the firelight, he saw armed guards at the mouth of the cave. Farther in, a small fire crackled, and beyond it sat the hunched figure of a man. Hylas couldn't see him clearly, but his shadow on the cave wall revealed him to be a big man with broad shoulders, long warrior braids, and a short, sharp beard.

Periphas put a hand on Hylas' shoulder and forced him to the ground. "On your knees before the true High Chieftain of Mycenae." Then he too went down on one knee, and bowed. "My lord," he said reverently. "It's just as you thought. It is the same boy."

The High Chieftain of Mycenae nodded. Rising to his feet, he turned and limped forward into the light, and stood looking down at Hylas.

Hylas' heart skipped a beat.

"Hello, Flea," said Akastos.

13

"Where's that lion of yours?" said Akastos, his face unreadable in the firelight.

"W-with Pirra," faltered Hylas, still reeling from the shock. "Somewhere called Dentra, looking for my sister."

"Why aren't you?"

"I went after Telamon. I thought he had the dagger. It was a trick. I only just escaped."

This isn't possible, he thought. Akastos the wanderer— Akastos the smith—Akastos the fugitive from the Angry Ones, who'd sworn to rid himself of Them and appease his brother's ghost by shedding the blood of a highborn Crow . . . *Akastos* is High Chieftain of Mycenae.

Hylas had last seen him in a hut in the Keftian mountains in the middle of a snowstorm. Then he'd worn tattered sheepskins and he'd been filthy and travel-stained. He was travel-stained now, but his tunic was fine linen, and he wore a kilt of gleaming scarlet leather. The sword-belt across his chest was tooled with gold, and from its scabbard jutted an ebony hilt banded with silver, the most precious metal of all.

Near the fire lay a massive shield of heavy white oxhide; on it, a great gilded lion gave a silent roar. There was a helmet covered in ivory plaques cut from boars' tusks, crested with a long white horsetail. There was armor fit for a god. Greaves, shoulder-guards, arm-pieces, breastplate: All were of burnished bronze, and figured with leaping stags and hunting lions.

Akastos had always had a warrior's build, and now he carried himself like one too. His long dark hair was in many braids threaded with gold wire; his beard was clipped close to the line of his jaw. But his eyes were as Hylas remembered: arrestingly light, and able to pierce you to your spirit and hold you spellbound.

With a start, Hylas realized that Akastos had spoken again. "I asked about Telamon," repeated Akastos. "Tell me you didn't leave him alive?"

That voice hadn't changed, either. It could be as smooth as water or as rough as granite, but always with an undertone of power that made you listen and obey.

"I could have killed him," said Hylas. "But I—I couldn't do it."

Behind him, Periphas gave an angry hiss. Akastos silenced him with a glance. "Helping the Crows has become something of a talent of yours, hasn't it, Hylas?"

Hylas flushed. He watched Akastos return to the fire and sit, signing him and Periphas to do the same.

Akastos took leaves from a pouch and chewed, washing them down with a pull from a two-handled wine cup of rough earthenware. The leaves were buckthorn, to ward off ghosts and the Angry Ones. So that was something else that hadn't changed.

"You're a problem I don't need, Flea," he growled. "My men want to kill you. I'm rather inclined to let them."

"But you can't!" Hylas blurted out. "You said once that our fates are intertwine—"

"I also said that whenever you turn up, things go wrong. And they usually do."

Hylas took a breath. "Give me five men and I'll go to Lapithos. I'll find a way to steal the dagger!"

Periphas snorted. Akastos stared at Hylas in disbelief. "After what you did, how can you *imagine* I'd set you free?"

"If you won't give me the men, I'll go on my own—"

"I don't think you understand how much trouble you're in," said Akastos. "Last summer on Thalakrea, I gave you the dagger to destroy—I had to, because you'd just lamed me in a fight!" He slapped the burn scar on his calf. "For reasons you've never explained, you failed to destroy it. And then this summer in Egypt, you *gave it to the Crows*!"

"I had to, or they'd have killed Pirra!"

"I don't care *why* you did it!" roared Akastos. "They got it back!" His voice rang through the cave. He rubbed his hand over his beard and said quietly, "The fact is, Hylas, my men are after your blood—and who can blame them?"

Hylas tried to swallow, but his mouth was too dry. "But—you're not after my blood, are you? Or—you,

Periphas?" He appealed to the younger man, who shifted uncomfortably.

A shadow crossed Akastos' hard features. Then he threw up his hands. "I don't know what to do with you, Flea! You get in my way, you cause endless trouble! But the truth is, you're part of what finally brought me back to Akea!"

Periphas threw him a startled glance.

Hylas risked a guess. "Was it something to do with Havoc?"

Akastos' lip curled. "I'd forgotten how clever you are. Yes. It was because of Havoc."

"Isn't that the lion cub he went looking for on Keftiu?" said Periphas.

"She's full-grown now," Hylas said proudly. "Oh, you should see her, Akastos—I mean, my lord—she's *beautiful,* and so strong!"

With a frown, Akastos regarded the great white shield at his feet, with its gilded lion. "Lions, always lions," he murmured. He turned to Periphas. "On Thalakrea, this boy fetches up at my smithy with a *lion cub* in tow. Then on Keftiu, the same lion leads him straight to me in the middle of a blizzard! You'd have to be an idiot to ignore omens like that."

Periphas was impressed. "Ah, now I understand: a lion, to bring back the Lion of Mycenae!"

Akastos nodded gravely. "I thought it meant that after all these years, the time had come for me to return. I thought that at last, I could lead my people to victory against the Crows—"

"And you *can*!" urged Periphas. "You *must*!"

"How?" Akastos flung back. Then to Hylas, "Do you know why I'm skulking in this cave, instead of fighting the Crows?"

"Um . . ."

"Because caves," he went on bitterly, "are the one place where the Angry Ones can't go! They're spirits of the air, Hylas, They can't get me down here under the earth—and that means my people can sleep in peace!"

He took another pull at his wine and wiped his mouth on the back of his hand. "Not long ago, I mustered what remains of our forces here in Messenia. They'd lost the battle for the north before I got here, but I thought that with me to lead them, we might still beat the Crows." He scowled. "We never even got within arrowshot. The night before, the Angry Ones came. You've been close to Them, Hylas, you can imagine what it was like: the chaos, the panic. Our beasts ran wild with terror, we lost a week's supplies when several stampeded over a cliff. How could I lead our men into battle when that would be the result?"

"But we'll take that chance!" cried Periphas. "Without you, we have none!"

"You don't know what They can do, Periphas," Akastos retorted. "You've never smelled Their charred flesh, or heard the crack of Their wings as They drop to the ground and come after you—snuffing you out in the dark, freezing your heart with dread . . ." His hand shook as he reached for his wine cup.

Silence in the cave. The fire crackled and spat.

Akastos squared his shoulders and skewered Hylas with his gaze. "All of which," he said drily, "has nothing to do with the question: What do I do with you?"

"Let me go," Hylas said promptly. "I'll find a way to get into Lapithos—"

"Oh, no, you've made enough trouble for me already, I'm not stupid enough to let you do it again!"

"So what are you going to do?"

Akastos regarded him with pity and regret, and Hylas' stomach disappeared. "I'm sorry, Flea. But you're bad luck. You've run out of chances."

Hylas opened his mouth to reply—but at that moment, there was a noise outside the cave and a guard ran in.

"A scout's just arrived, my lord," he said, dropping to one knee. "From Lykonia! He says it's urgent!"

⊰⊷⊷⊷

The scout had been running for days. He was gray with dust and his feet were bleeding; the guards had to help him to the fire. He collapsed before Akastos, who wouldn't let him speak till he'd had a cup of wine mixed with barley and goats' cheese, and made a start on a steaming bowl of gruel.

The man's story came in bursts between ravenous mouthfuls. Pharax was moving west across the Lykonian plains, burning villages and driving the remaining rebels before him. His army was large and disciplined, the rebels badly outnumbered. Meanwhile, on the other side of the mountains, Telamon's forces were heading *east,* making for Lykonia through the pass on the south slope of Mount Lykas.

"A pincer movement." Akastos nodded slowly. "Pharax will attack the Lykonian rebels from one side, Telamon from the other." He ground his palms together. "They'll be caught in the middle and crushed."

"They might have a chance if we could reach them in time," said Periphas.

"Yes but how?" growled Akastos. "We're in Messenia, on the other side of the mountains—and we can't take the pass because Telamon's forces are already there, or will be soon. And before you suggest that we ambush him, Periphas, we'd never reach them in time."

"My lord, that's not all," panted the scout. "It's said that Pharax bears the dagger of Koronos openly in battle!"

"But that can't be!" Hylas burst out. "Surely it's in Lapithos?"

The man noticed him for the first time and blinked.

"Go on," Akastos commanded.

"The dagger *was* in Lapithos," said the man, "but from what we hear, we think Koronos may have sent it to Pharax, to rally his men. If that's true . . ." He shuddered. "No one could stand against him! With the dagger, he'll be invincible!"

"How do you know for sure that it really is the dagger?" said Akastos.

"I—I don't, my lord," admitted the scout. "No one knows for sure."

"Which is exactly what Koronos wants," murmured Akastos. "He sows doubts and fears, it all helps Pharax. The rebels in Lykonia won't stand a chance."

"Unless we reach them first!" exploded Periphas. "If we get to them before Pharax, we can make a stand *together*! Dagger or no dagger, with you to lead us, we could defeat them!"

"But there's no *time*!" spat Akastos. "We can't go by the pass to the south, because of Telamon—and it'd take at least five days to get through the mountains any other way!"

"No it won't," said Hylas.

All heads turned toward him.

"Who *is* this?" said the scout.

Akastos' eyes bored into Hylas'. "What are you talking about?"

"I know a way to get your men through the mountains in time," said Hylas. "*And* I know how to keep the Angry Ones away, so that you can lead us into battle."

"How could you possibly achieve all that?" said Akastos with terrifying quietness.

Hylas hesitated. "If I tell you, will you let me go?"

"This is no time for *bargaining*!"

Hylas took a deep breath. "All right. First, the Angry Ones. Pirra's gone to a peak shrine, somewhere called Dentra, there's a wisewoman—"

"I already know about the wisewoman," snarled Akastos.

"But do you know that it's Hekabi?"

The High Chieftain went still.

"Who's Hekabi?" said Periphas.

"A wisewoman from Thalakrea," said Hylas. "Very powerful. Last summer, she gave Akastos a charm to mask him from the Angry Ones—and it *worked,* Akastos, you know it did! I was with you in Kreon's stronghold when he summoned Them, and *They never sensed that you were there!* Hekabi could do it again!"

"If we can find her in time," muttered Akastos, rubbing his beard. "Dentra's not all that far, so maybe we could, but even if it worked—*even if*—we couldn't get through the mountains in time to join forces with the others against the Crows."

"Yes we could!" insisted Hylas. "The pass Telamon's taking isn't the only one! I know another." He glanced at the scout, then back to Akastos. "You said it'd take five days to cross the mountains into Lykonia. I can get us there in two."

14

"Not far now," panted Pirra as she scrambled up the slope.

Above her, Havoc glanced back and waited for her to catch up. It was two days since the lioness had saved Pirra's life by fighting off the lion, but although the gash in her shoulder remained oozing and smelly, she seemed much happier. She'd stopped pining for Hylas, and had been staying close to Pirra: as if she felt it her duty to protect her.

It was Echo who occupied Pirra's every waking thought. The Marsh Dwellers' medicine clearly didn't work on falcons. Echo was desperately ill, and couldn't last much longer. To keep her warm, Pirra had tucked her inside her tunic, where she made a bulky yet pathetically light bulge and lay frighteningly still, her only sign of life an occasional feeble scratch of talons.

Now and then, Pirra was assailed by a wave of dizziness; she knew that she was feeling what the falcon felt. Sounds fell away, and the bright air darkened to a pinpoint as her spirit drifted with Echo's in a blaze of fever.

"Nearly there, Echo," she mumbled. "We'll find Hekabi; she'll make you better, I promise!"

Olive trees shone silver in the last of the Sun, and the wind stirred thistles and dry yellow grass: They were nearing the top of Dentra Mountain. The river they'd been following upstream had dwindled to a gurgling trickle, and only a belt of tall pines separated them from the peak.

Pirra could feel that the shrine was very close. The air was filled with a strange, low buzzing, just beyond the edge of hearing. What if Hekabi was gone? Or if it wasn't Hekabi at all, but some stranger who refused to help?

And even if it *was* Hekabi, *would* she help? When Pirra had known her on Thalakrea, she'd been ruthless and secretive. Sometimes her spells had been real, sometimes fake; it had been hard to tell the difference. The one thing that had never altered was Hekabi's all-consuming love for her fiery island home—which the Crows, in their greed for bronze, had destroyed.

Havoc trotted down to her and gently nosed the falcon-shaped bulge in Pirra's tunic. Echo didn't stir. Pirra quickened her pace.

The buzzing grew louder. Havoc, once more waiting for Pirra at the edge of the pines, didn't seem scared, only wary.

The slopes below had been shrill with swallows, but up here there were no birds. Pine needles muffled Pirra's footsteps as she entered the cool, sharp-scented shade.

The buzzing was eerie and unsettling, it seemed to be everywhere and nowhere. With a jolt, Pirra saw that it was coming from the trees themselves. They were alive with bees: thousands of them going about their mysterious lives in their realm among the branches, between earth and sky.

The Sun sank behind the western peaks, and the buzzing turned slightly threatening. Wind chilled the sweat on Pirra's skin as she left the trees and stepped out onto naked rock. Dentra's jagged gray peak reared above her.

Keftian peak shrines had altars and bulls' horns, but Dentra had only the black mouth of a small cave at the base of the peak, half hidden by a fig tree hung with ragged offerings. The stream trickled from the cave; the shrine must lie within.

"Hekabi?" Pirra called softly.

Behind her, the buzzing rose angrily: The bees didn't like her speaking out loud.

"Hekabi!" she whispered. "It's me! Pirra!"

No answer: only the bees and the wind soughing in the pines, and the echoing gurgle of the unseen spring. Pirra touched the bulge in her tunic where Echo drifted in fever. If she couldn't find Hekabi, the falcon would die.

Beside her, Havoc caught some scent and bounded off downhill. Pirra didn't call her back, she knew the lioness would stay within earshot; besides, calling would anger the bees.

She glimpsed a wisp of smoke drifting from the cave. Her heart quickened. There was someone in there.

"Hold on, Echo," she panted. "If she's in there, I'll *make* her cure you!"

But at the cave mouth, she faltered. One of the offerings on the fig tree was a dead crow, dangling by its wing. The bird had been ripped messily open, as if in fury; its eye sockets were seething with maggots. Stepping sideways to avoid it, Pirra nearly trod in an earthenware basin on the ground. It was brimful with blood, gone sludgy, and swarming with flies.

After the heat of the mountainside, the inside of the cave felt cold. It was dark, except for three dim points of light a few paces in, and it rang with the voice of the spring. Smoke stung Pirra's eyes: not the heady scent of incense, but foul fumes that made her gorge rise.

"Hekabi?" she whispered.

Hekabi, Hekabi, whispered the cave.

Bent double and groping blindly, Pirra stumbled past a small black pool that must be the spring. She touched wet rocks. Her palms came away dark. It smelled like blood.

As her eyes adjusted to the gloom, she saw that the cave was high enough for her to stand upright. All around, in every crack and crevice, someone had placed little clay creatures: bulls, foxes, pine martens, snakes, frogs— all facing inward, their painted eyes gazing past her to a small three-legged offering-table of gray plaster, set at the shrine's stony heart.

Pirra caught her breath. Everything about this offering was wrong. The table was upside down, its three legs pointing at the roof, and to each of these had been tied a smoldering stick tipped not with incense, but reeking dung. The offerings themselves were on spikes stuck in the table's underbelly. One was a scrap of blood-crusted bandage wound around the shriveled corpse of a viper. The second was a fragment of a fine drinking cup, cradled in the ragged wing of a bat. The third was a narrow braid of dark hair with a small clay disc at one end, twisted around a dead scorpion.

Pirra's skin crawled. *A curse*, she thought. *This is a curse.*

At that moment, she became aware of a low muttering beneath the voice of the spring: hissing, spitting, filling the air with venom.

In the shadows at the back of the cave, something moved. Pirra took in a shock of matted gray hair and a malevolent gray face rushing toward her. "Get out!" it screeched in a blast of fetid breath. *"Get out get out get out!"*

Pirra ducked. Gray fingers clawed the air by her throat. "It's me, Pirra!" she cried.

The creature froze. Its wild gaze fixed on the crescent-moon scar on Pirra's cheek.

"You!" rasped Hekabi.

———

"The spirits have abandoned me," muttered Hekabi, pacing up and down outside the cave. "Nothing works, nothing, and now this girl . . . What does it *mean*?"

"Echo's sick," said Pirra. "You have to save her!"

Hekabi flung her a distracted look and went on pacing.

Pirra was appalled. The wisewoman was unrecognizable. She'd been almost handsome before, with strong, ageless features. Now she was ragged, skeletally thin, and caked from head to foot in gray clay. The ritual burn scars on her forearms that all Islanders bore had become fresh scabs, clawed open in mourning for her vanished home. Her dark eyes darted feverishly, and she gave off rage like heat from a fire.

Pirra was horrified. If grief for her lost homeland had sent the wisewoman mad, then Echo was doomed.

"Nothing works," muttered Hekabi, twisting her hands till the knuckles cracked. "Something's missing, but *what*?"

"Hekabi, *listen*! Echo's dying, you've got to save her!"

"What do I care?" snarled the wisewoman. "Nothing matters but destroying the Crows—and it can't be done by weapons alone!"

"You used to care," said Pirra. "You were kind to Havoc on Thalakrea!"

The wisewoman flinched as if the memory hurt. "Darkness and pain, nothing left . . . Hekabi lives only to crush the Crows."

Pirra thought of the upside-down offering in the cave. She remembered the little clay disc at the end of the braid. Suddenly, she knew. That hair was Telamon's.

"You're trying to curse the Crows," she said. "That potsherd—it belonged to Koronos, didn't it? He only ever uses a vessel once, then it's smashed. And that bloody bandage, it must have belonged to Pharax—"

"But why won't it *take*?" shouted Hekabi. "Hekabi's tried everything but nothing *works*! Something's missing, but *what*?"

"I know a bit about curses," Pirra said reluctantly. "I did one in Egypt. It drew the crocodiles that killed Alekto."

Hekabi swung around. "That was you?"

Pirra nodded. "I'll help you. But first you *must* help Echo."

Hekabi hesitated. "Show," she commanded.

Gently, Pirra drew the falcon from inside her tunic. Echo felt terrifyingly light. Her head drooped, and through her yellow eyelids, only a dark slit showed. Her beautiful slate-gray wings were dull, and her pale flecked breast felt emaciated. With a clutch of terror, Pirra wondered if even Hekabi could save her.

The wisewoman ran one filthy clay-caked finger down the falcon's breast, and frowned. "This bird has power. Where's she from?"

"Keftiu."

"But where?"

"Taka Zimi. That's a peak sanctuary on Mount—"

"I know where it is." Hekabi was pacing again, and her eyes had a hectic glitter. "That's *it*," she muttered. "Yes, to make it work, I must have help from *many* lands, wherever the Crows have defiled! This sacred bird from Keftiu—"

"*No!*" cried Pirra. "You can't have Echo!"

"Not for sacrifice," spat Hekabi. "A feather will do!"

"Not even that, the shock might kill her!"

Hekabi went on pacing as if she hadn't heard. "Many lands, yes, that's *it*!" She halted. "But what about Thalakrea? I have nothing from my own land!"

"What about those obsidian beads you used to wear," said Pirra, cradling Echo protectively. "Or your seeing-stone, or sulfur from the Mountain of Fire—"

"All gone," moaned the wisewoman, her face twisted in anguish. "Lost in the scramble to escape, nothing *left*! The curse will *fail*!"

"No it won't," said Pirra in an altered voice. Wrenching open her pouch, she pulled out her little ivory comb and flung it at Hekabi's feet. "There, that's from Egypt. And here . . ." She threw down her last gold poppy-head. "That's from Keftiu, from the House of the Goddess itself; it's far more powerful than a feather!"

Hekabi pounced on the things and snatched them to her breast. "What about Thalakrea?"

Pirra's thoughts darted. "If I give you something from there, then in return, you must *swear* to help Echo."

Hekabi's eyes narrowed with suspicion. "You have something from *my Island*? How can that be, when it no longer exists! The Crows angered the Lady of Fire and She blasted it from the Sea!"

"I have something," insisted Pirra. "But first, swear to cure Echo!"

"Not till you show me."

Pirra cleared her throat and called. She waited. She called again.

Hekabi caught movement on the slope below—and gasped.

Havoc stood at the edge of the pines. Her ears were pricked, and she glanced warily from Pirra to Hekabi as she sniffed the wisewoman's scent. In the last of the Sun, her fur blazed golden, and her great black-rimmed eyes were filled with light.

"I'll give you one tuft of her fur," said Pirra, "but no more. And first, you must *swear* to cure Echo—and not hurt Havoc."

"*Hurt* her?" whispered Hekabi, sinking to her knees. Tears were streaming down her cheeks, carving runnels in the cracked gray clay. "*Hurt* a sacred creature of the Lady of Fire?"

"Swear," repeated Pirra.

"I swear," murmured Hekabi. "By my lost Island—by the Lady of Fire Herself—I swear." She drew a ragged breath and held out her hands. "Give me the falcon. I'll do what I can. Although I think it may already be too late."

15

"Sometimes—when she's flying," faltered Pirra, "it feels as if I'm flying too. I'm riding the wind, I can feel it under my wings, and I can see the prey, incredibly far below. I'm with her in every swoop and glide, every twist and somersault and dive. But now . . ." She pinched the bridge of her nose to hold back the tears. "Now there's nothing but darkness and a tiny point of light, very far away. I'm so weak I can hardly move my wings—I mean, Echo can't—and she's frightened and *angry,* she doesn't understand that she's sick. All she knows is that she can't fly, and for a falcon that's the worst thing ever . . ."

Hekabi sat cross-legged with the falcon in her lap. Slipping her fingers under one wing, she felt Echo's breast. "Too thin. The muscles are wasted." She wiped foam from Echo's beak and sniffed. "Smells foul. What medicine have you tried?"

Pirra told her about the Marsh Dwellers' black powder. "I don't know what it was, the boy who gave it to me couldn't speak."

Something flickered in Hekabi's brown eyes. "Sounds like ground poppy seeds."

"Well, it doesn't work on falcons."

Hekabi touched Echo's dull yellow foot and frowned. "Hot where she should be cool—"

"I *know* all this!" Pirra burst out. "I *know* her feathers have lost their shine, I *know* she can't stop shivering! What are you going to *do* about it?"

Echo half opened one eye and gave a croak that twisted Pirra's heart. "Can you save her?"

"I told you, I don't know. Have you meat?"

Pirra handed her the smelly little pouch in which she saved scraps for Echo, and Hekabi took out a shred of pigeon. From her battered goatskin bag, she drew a stoppered cow horn and tipped a few drops of greenish liquid into her palm.

"What's that?" Pirra said suspiciously.

"Mustard seed, garlic, a few other things."

Havoc pushed in her muzzle, and the wisewoman gently moved her aside. Having coated the meat in the potion, she prized open Echo's beak and tucked it in, lightly massaging under the chin till the falcon swallowed. "First, I must put her to sleep. The deepest of sleeps . . . to the very border of death."

Pirra licked her lips. "And then? Are you going to do a spell?"

"No. You are. Lie down." Hekabi held out the cow horn. "Drink."

"What?"

"I must put you to sleep too. So that you can go after her spirit and bring her back."

———

The falcon is burning hot and aching all over. Everything sounds fuzzy and unfamiliar and she can't see, except for a tiny spark of brightness, very far away. She knows she has to reach this, although she doesn't know why, and she's too weak to fly.

Somehow, she finds a way to spread her wings, so that the wind can do the lifting for her. It isn't proper flying, she's merely gliding, but it's all she can manage because she's so weak.

Glancing down, she spots the she-lion very far below. The she-lion is racing after her, glancing up now and then, to check that she's still there. The she-lion is doing her best—in fact, the falcon has never seen her move so fast, her paws scarcely touching the ground as she hurtles around pines and leaps over rocks—but like all earthbound creatures, she's no match for the Wind, and with a pang, the falcon sees her slipping behind.

The bright point is growing steadily bigger as the Wind spirals upward, carrying the falcon toward it. The earth is dropping away fast. She doesn't want to leave it, and she knows that if she goes too high, she will never get back.

Now someone else is coming after her. She sees who it is and her spirit soars: It's the girl, and she's *flying*. Her strange beakless face is pale and intent, and her long hair is streaming behind her, dark locks shot through with brilliant glints of purple and red. She is utterly determined to stop the falcon leaving her. The falcon feels the strength of the girl's love, pulling her back.

But being human, the girl is no good at flying. Slower than a pigeon, clumsier than a fledgling, she's wobbling about on the Wind, and when she comes to a bumpy bit, she nearly falls off. The falcon wants to slow down, so that the girl can catch up, but the Wind won't let her.

The girl is calling her back in her deep, slow human voice. It sounds muffled, and beneath it the falcon feels the heat of the girl's fiery spirit, desperately tugging at hers. And yet—like the she-lion—the girl is slipping behind. It isn't *fair*. The falcon doesn't *want* the Wind to carry her toward the light. Once she reaches it, she will never return. She will never see the girl again.

With an enormous effort, the falcon tilts the tip of one wing feather, trying to shift herself sideways, off the Wind. It isn't enough, and she hasn't the strength to do it again— but somehow, she does. And again . . . and again. With an ungainly lurch, she topples off the Wind.

Mustering the last of her strength, she draws in her wings, tucks in her head and feet—and plummets back to earth.

Toward the girl.

⚊⚊

Pirra woke with a thumping headache, rolled onto her side, and threw up.

Slumping back against the fig tree's knobbly roots,

she lay squinting at the morning Sun through the leaves. Shreds from yesterday drifted back, and she started up again. "Echo! Is she—"

"Alive," said Hekabi. "All she needs now is food and rest."

The falcon was perched on a tree root near Pirra's head. Her feathers were freshly preened, there was no foam around her beak, and the sparkle had returned to her large dark eyes.

Weakly, Pirra stretched out her hand. The falcon sidled toward her and hopped onto her shoulder. She took a lock of Pirra's hair in her beak, and gave it swift little preening tugs.

Pirra's eyes stung. Echo hadn't done that since they'd left the marshes. With her finger, she stroked the falcon's scaly foot. It was no longer feverishly hot, but cool, and a bright, clear yellow.

"I'm so glad you're better," whispered Pirra.

Embarrassed, Echo glanced away. Then she stretched her wings behind her, bobbed up and down, and sicked up a pellet.

"Here," said Pirra, offering Hekabi the neat oval of crunched-up pigeon feathers. "To help with the curse."

Hekabi took it without a word and went on cramming things into her goatskin bag. During the night, she'd washed off all the clay, and now that her hair was brown again, the white streak showed at her temple. She looked much more her old self, although her eyes still had that hectic glitter. She'd brought the offering-table from the cave, and was busy wrapping the three pieces of the curse in fig leaves.

Pirra asked what she was doing, and Hekabi told her that the first part of the curse was finished—now she had to send it to the Crows. "For that we need to go to the other side of the peak."

"We?"

"You owe me a tuft of lion fur."

Pirra didn't reply. For the first time since Echo had fallen ill, she'd remembered why she'd been looking for Hekabi. What would Hylas say if he knew that she'd forgotten all about Issi?

They followed a goat trail that circled the peak: Pirra carrying the offering-table with Echo perched on her shoulder, and Havoc following. Now and then, Hekabi turned aside to gather herbs or firewood, examining each stick and flinging most of them away.

Pirra thought of the three grisly offerings: Telamon's hair, Koronos' potsherd, and Pharax's bandage. "The pieces of the curse," she said carefully. "How did you get them?"

Hekabi didn't answer.

"Was it—did the shadow thief help you?"

Still no reply.

"Hekabi, it's important. The shadow thief . . . The Marsh Dwellers think you made it in a spell, but Hylas—he thinks it might be his sister."

"Why?" Hekabi said irritably without turning around.

"Well, because . . . He says she's good at stealing, and her favorite creatures are frogs, and the Marsh Dwellers said the shadow thief leaves little clay frogs. And I saw one in the cave—"

"Don't talk to me about frogs!" snapped Hekabi. "All I care about is the curse!"

"You cared about Hylas once, you said he's the Outsider in the Oracle; and you prophesied to the Marsh Dwellers about him: *Fin, feather, and fur*—"

But Hekabi had gone striding ahead.

Shortly after noon, they reached the eastern side of Dentra peak, and Hekabi halted at a rocky ledge. Beneath them was a dizzying drop; above them loomed the dark-red heights of Mount Lykas.

"The Crows call its tallest fang the Ancestor Peak," Hekabi said grimly. "That's where they dug the Tomb of the House of Koronos, long ago. If I can send the curse all the way to their Tomb, I can blight them forever."

Pirra threw her a glance. "How do you know this? Have you been there?"

She gave a crooked smile. "I didn't need to."

"Why not? Did the shadow thief tell you? *Was* it Hylas' sister? Her name's Issi, Hekabi, and she grew up on Mount Lykas, so she'd know all about it!"

"Stop plaguing me, I know nothing of sisters! And if I did have a 'shadow thief' to help me, that's in the past! It's time to complete the curse. Give me the lion fur."

"Hekabi *please*—"

"The fur!"

Setting her teeth, Pirra placed Echo on the branch of a thorn tree. She didn't have to summon Havoc; the lioness seemed to sense that she was needed, and leaned against her while Pirra cut a tuft from her scruff. Havoc gave her a rasping lick on the cheek to show that she didn't mind, then slumped under the tree and yawned.

Pirra noticed that the gash on the lioness' shoulder was smeared with a greenish poultice that gave off a sharp, clean herbal tang. "Did you do that?" she asked Hekabi.

"No," muttered Hekabi. "Give me the fur!"

"Then who did?"

"How do I know? Give it here!"

"Was it the shadow thief?"

"Give me the fur!"

Seething, Pirra did as she was told.

"Watch," commanded Hekabi. "Listen. Don't say a word."

First, the wisewoman woke a fire. The wood she'd gathered was mastic, and caught quickly: Soon tarry smoke was stinging Pirra's eyes.

Squatting and rocking back and forth, Hekabi threw Pirra's little ivory comb into the flames, then Echo's pellet and the piece of Keftian gold—and then, with reverence, the tuft of Havoc's fur . . . Lastly, she cast in the three pieces of the curse.

Smoke twisted into the air. The curse-fire crackled and spat.

Havoc put her head between her paws. Pirra saw flames dancing in the lioness' golden eyes.

Hekabi sat cross-legged with her palms upward on her knees and began to chant. *"Bind, bury, and banish . . . May the cursed ones cower in darkness for eternity . . . May the cursed ones have nothing to eat but dust for bread, and clay for meat . . ."*

Echo peered down from her branch. Suddenly, she swiveled her head right around, as if she'd spotted something in the distance. A moment later, a vast twittering cloud of starlings swept across the sky. The flock was so dense that the birds darkened the Sun like cloudshadow, and their wings created their own breeze, stirring Pirra's hair and wafting the smoke from the curse-fire toward the Ancestor Peak.

Closer and closer drifted the smoke. *"Bind, bury, and banish . . ."* chanted Hekabi.

Pirra's scalp prickled. Havoc sprang up, turning her head to follow something Pirra couldn't see: something that rose from the fire and flew swiftly through the air toward the Ancestor Peak.

A violent wind came roaring in, scattering the starlings and blowing the smoke back in Pirra's face.

Hekabi stopped chanting. She sat rigid, her fists clenched.

"Did it work?" whispered Pirra. "Did the curse reach the Ancestor Peak?"

Hekabi drew a ragged breath. "Only the gods know for sure . . . But time will tell."

They sat in silence until Pirra couldn't bear it anymore. "Hekabi, you *must* tell me—for Hylas. Is the shadow thief Issi?"

"The shadow thief?" Hekabi frowned, as if her mind had been far away. "Issi? Until you came, I'd never even heard that name!"

Pirra swallowed. "I don't believe you. You can't have gathered those things by yourself, and you can't know all about the Ancestor Peak if you've never been there! If Issi *is* the shadow thief, you have to tell me where she is!"

Hekabi turned on her. "The shadow thief is a *boy*, Pirra! He's a *boy*! I know nothing about any girl called Issi!"

16

Issi had thoroughly enjoyed watching the wisewoman do the curse. After all, she'd helped make it happen. She'd risked her life stealing what was needed, and she'd put that little clay frog in the cave, to keep an eye on things for her.

From her hiding place among the rocks, she'd watched the wisewoman feeding the Crows' things to the curse-fire, and given a silent cheer when it ate Telamon's hair. *Serves you right, you traitor,* she'd told him in her head, picturing Lapithos crashing down in flames and the Crows fleeing in terror. *Burn, burn! This is for Hylas, wherever he is—and for Scram, and for everyone you've killed . . .*

Now the wisewoman and the girl called Pirra were heading down the mountain. Issi's belly tightened with excitement. Soon, she would make herself known to the girl. The girl knew Hylas—Issi had gathered that from what she'd overheard—so she'd be delighted to see Issi. "*Issi!*" she would cry. "Can it really be you? Hylas will be so *happy*! He's never stopped looking for you, let's go and find him right now!"

That was what Issi wanted to happen; but out of habit, she stayed hidden as she followed them. *Careful, Issi, you don't yet know for sure that you can trust this girl. Remember what's kept you alive all this time: Stay hidden, say nothing, trust no one. Never reveal who you are.*

Slipping between the pine trees, she didn't notice she was being stalked until a powerful blow knocked her legs from under her and sent her sprawling in the bracken. For a moment, she lay winded. Then she broke into a grin.

Havoc stood over her, play-growling and nuzzling her tummy with her furry muzzle. Giggling, Issi pummeled the lioness' chest with both fists, then squirmed out from under and flung her arms around Havoc's neck. They rubbed cheeks, the lioness making groany noises that meant she was glad she'd found her new friend again.

Issi was pleased that the gash in Havoc's shoulder was healing so well that she wouldn't have to smear on any more of her salve. And clearly the lioness was no longer worried about the falcon: She was ready to play. Remembering something Hylas used to do, Issi cut some switches, swiftly wove them into a rough wicker ball, and tossed it to her.

Havoc *loved* it, seeming to know at once what it was for, and batting it back with her forepaw. Issi threw it farther and they raced for it. Havoc won, and after an uproarious play-fight, they collapsed in a comfortable, panting heap. Havoc flung one huge paw across Issi's chest, and with a laugh, she struggled to push it off. Her laugh sounded unfamiliar. She hadn't laughed since the coming of the Crows.

To stop the memories from breaking through, she pressed her face into Havoc's fur and sniffed her musky lion smell. It didn't work. She felt as if she wasn't snuggling against the lioness, but Scram . . .

The day the Crows attacked, it had been fiercely hot, with clouds piling up over Mount Lykas. "Storm on the way," Hylas had said as they pitched camp in a cave on the western peak. "I'm going to the stream to cool off. Don't let that squirrel burn!"

Issi rolled her eyes. "When have I *ever* done that?"

"Day before yesterday."

"I did not!"

With a wave of his hand, he headed down toward the stream. "It wasn't *burned*!" she yelled after him, but he only grinned in his infuriating way.

Muttering, Issi wandered off to gather asphodel roots.

Scram's warning *whuff*! stopped her in her tracks. The next moment, she heard his frantic barks.

Drawing her knife, she rushed back to camp. She heard men's voices and ducked into a thicket. She caught a strange, bitter stink of ash.

Scram's barks cut off. Issi heard a whimper—then silence. She crept forward. She blinked.

Three goats lay with their throats cut, while seven men bristling with weapons ransacked the camp. They wore black rawhide armor and long black cloaks, and their faces were gray and inhuman with ash. Then she saw Scram. There was a roaring in her ears. She saw his big tough paws and the arrow jutting from his flank.

Her thoughts tumbled over each other. Hylas. He was down at the stream, he didn't know. *"Hylas!"* she screamed. *"Warriors! Run!"*

She darted back into the thicket with the warriors crashing after her. They were bigger than her, they couldn't get through. Somehow, she worked her way around and slipped between the rocks into the back of the cave: They'd already searched in here, they wouldn't search again . . .

Then she saw Hylas. He was on the other side of camp, crouching behind a juniper bush. He felt her gaze, and for an instant that burned into her memory, their eyes locked. She knew what he was telling her: *Don't move. Stay hidden.* Then with terrifying purposefulness, he stepped into the open and yelled at the Crows: "Over here!"

Seven ash-gray faces turned toward him. In horror, Issi saw arrows nocked to bows, swords and spears brandished as the warriors went thundering after him.

The last she'd ever seen of her brother, he'd been racing down the slope with the Crows in pursuit, their long black cloaks flying like wings . . .

Havoc grunted in her sleep and rolled onto her back, with all four paws flopping outward. Issi snuggled closer against her furry flank.

Hylas had been an infuriating older brother and they'd squabbled all the time, but she'd always known that he would look after her. *If you ever get lost,* he used to say, *stay where you are and wait. I will find you.* And he always had.

But not this time.

Issi didn't remember much of what had happened right after the attack. She'd waited for ages, then left a message for Hylas at the rock at the top of the pass. She'd caught sight of the Sea far below, and the vast green marshes.

There'll be frogs down there, she'd thought numbly. And no dogs. After what had happened to Scram, she couldn't bear to be anywhere near dogs.

As she'd made her way down, she'd seen terrible things. The Crows were hunting Outsiders. That was why they were after her and Hylas. When she'd reached the marshes, she'd smeared herself in mud and stolen some fish skin to hide her fair hair, she'd tied a brown band around her forehead: there. Now she was no longer Issi the Outsider, she was a Marsh Dweller boy.

The Marsh Dwellers had given her food and shelter, but she hadn't trusted them. Since the Crows had attacked, she hadn't spoken to anyone, and now she found that she couldn't; her voice no longer worked. She didn't care. It was better that way.

The only times she'd felt safe were when she was by herself, listening to the frogs, or watching the fishes sliding through the green water. And the one thing she'd never doubted was that Hylas was still alive and still looking for her. All through two winters, and that terrible spring when the Sun was blotted out, she'd told herself: *He will come back. He will find me. Until he does, I must stay alive and do what I can to fight the Crows.*

And she had. When the wisewoman came to the marshes, Issi had liked her, because she lived only to destroy the Crows. Issi hadn't let down her guard, not even with her, yet when the wisewoman left the marshes, she'd followed, and helped her steal things for the curse. But when the wisewoman had caked herself in clay, and couldn't get the curse to work, Issi had left her and returned to the coast.

Then a few days ago, everything had changed. At the edge of the marshes, she'd encountered a stranger, a girl with a scar on her cheek, a falcon on her wrist, and a lioness at her side.

Issi wasn't afraid of any wild creature, but even she had been surprised at how easily she'd made friends with the lioness. They'd been drawn to each other, maybe because the lioness was miserable, and Issi knew what that was like.

The day after they'd met, Issi had hidden among the reeds and watched the girl kneel beside the lioness. "I know, Havoc," the girl had said sadly. "You miss Hylas, and so do I."

Issi had been stunned. It was the first time in two summers that she'd heard her brother's name. The joy was so sharp, she felt as if her chest had split open. *Hylas is alive and this girl knows him . . .*

Issi had wanted to burst from her hiding place and race over to her: "Where is he? Where is he?" But long habits of caution had kept her hidden. And to her consternation, she'd gathered that Hylas had been here, in the marshes—and had only just left. Issi had been in despair. She had missed her brother by a whisker.

But she hadn't waited for him all this time to give up now. Follow this girl, she'd told herself. Follow this girl and you will find him.

Again, Havoc rolled over and flung one heavy forepaw across Issi's body. Issi stroked the huge rough pad, and felt the lioness' hot, sawing breath on her face. She knew she could trust Havoc as surely as she trusted her brother, but she wasn't so certain about Pirra. And trusting no one had saved her life.

In that first awful time after the Crows attacked the camp, she'd gone in search of Telamon. Telamon was their friend, he would know what to do.

It had been sheer chance that she'd seen him before he'd seen her. She'd been plodding along a goat trail, footsore, hungry, and frightened, when she'd caught the stink of ash on the wind, and flung herself behind a thorn bush.

She remembered hearing the creak of leather as the pounding feet came nearer, then a nightmare of black armor and weapons had swept into view. Their leader was a monster of darkness. His armor wasn't rawhide, but some metal that gleamed like copper—only darker and angrier. *Bronze,* she'd thought. That must be bronze.

He'd been level with her hiding place when he'd called a halt. She hadn't been able to see his face, just an eye-slit between his bronze throat-guard that masked nose and mouth and his boar's-tusk helmet, crested with black horsetail. Only his hair, in a warrior's snake-like braids, had shown that he was human.

"Clear the mountains," he'd said in a hollow voice that had made her think of cold places that never saw the Sun. "No Outsider must remain alive." Then he'd turned to someone behind him. "I can count on you. Yes?"

". . . Yes, Uncle," a voice had replied. Then Telamon—*Telamon*—had moved into view.

Issi had felt sick. *Telamon is one of them. Telamon is a Crow . . .*

Havoc yawned cavernously and heaved herself to her feet, and nose-nudged Issi's belly. Issi pushed the great muzzle away. She felt shaky inside. The memories were bitter in her mouth.

Havoc snuffed the air, threw Issi a friendly glance, then ambled off through the trees.

She's going to find Pirra, thought Issi.

Slowly, she retrieved her waterskin and ax, and checked that she still had her knife, strike-fire, and slingshot. Then she headed after the lioness.

On that day two summers ago when she'd seen Telamon, she'd learned something that had kept her alive ever since: *People lie. You can't trust them.*

She would follow Pirra, because Pirra might lead her to Hylas. But it was not yet time to reveal herself to her.

Pirra and the wisewoman had camped beside a stream that splashed noisily over rocks. The wisewoman was waking a fire, and Pirra was feeding the falcon scraps of meat. Creeping nearer, Issi caught snatches of talk above the chatter of the stream.

". . . if you feel like that," said the wisewoman wryly, "why did you leave him?"

Issi's heart quickened. Were they talking about Hylas?

"I didn't," said Pirra. "He wanted us to split up because . . ." She turned her head, and her words were drowned by the stream. ". . . not only that," she said, turning back. "Ever since Thalakrea, he's been having visions."

The wisewoman stopped what she was doing. "What kind of visions?" she said sharply.

"Ghosts, spirits. It first happened last spring, when we were on Keftiu, then in Egypt they got stronger; now he even sees gods." She frowned. "Hylas is convinced that he's become dangerous to be with. I think that's why he sent me away, to keep the three of us safe."

"Are you a mated pair?" said the wisewoman.

Pirra flushed. "That's nothing to do with you!"

The wisewoman snorted. "But you'd like to be."

Pirra's flush deepened. "Of course I would. I think he feels the same way . . . No, I don't *think*, I *know*. In Egypt he would have given his life to save me. But he's never *said* anything," she burst out, "and now I don't know where he is, and I might never see him again!"

There was a booming in Issi's head. This girl had been

with Hylas for ages—in places called Keftiu, and Thalakrea, and Egypt—where *he would have given his life for her* . . .

Until now, Issi had never felt truly alone: She'd always had the thought of Hylas to keep her company, and the belief that one day they would be together again, the two of them against the world, just as it was before. Now, with brutal suddenness, that was gone. Even if she found him, this girl, Pirra, would be in the way. She would come between them. Nothing would be as it was before.

"Havoc!" called the girl. "Havoc, where are you?"

The lioness pushed past Issi and bounded toward the camp. Numbly, Issi watched her go. The pain in her chest was so bad, she could hardly breathe. *The three of us,* Pirra had said: girl, falcon, and lion. Hylas had a new family now. How could Issi fit into that?

The lioness paused and glanced back at her: *Aren't you coming too?*

Slowly, Issi shook her head. She backed away. Then she turned and ran.

17

The last time Hylas had been in the secret pass, he'd been with Issi. It had been winter, and they'd fought a mock battle with icicles for swords. He'd let her win, and she'd been furious.

"You're not *trying*!" she'd shrieked. "You've got to *try*, or it's not a proper fight!" Her sharp little face had been contorted with rage as she'd hopped up and down, but then Scram had butted in, swinging his tail, and she'd shot Hylas a withering glare and play-fought the dog instead . . .

Hylas paused at a turn in the trail and waited for the rebels to catch up. At last, he was back on Mount Lykas. The secret pass wound through a confusion of spurs and gullies on its northern flank. Far overhead, its triple fangs were lost in cloud, and around him every crag and tree was steeped in memories. He quickened his pace. Why couldn't the rebels go any faster?

It was the second day that he'd been guiding Akastos' forces through the secret pass, and he was desperate to reach the other side, where the Lykonian rebels were camped. Had the scouts found Pirra and Hekabi on Dentra? For all he knew, they might already be at camp. For all he knew, they might have brought Issi . . .

"Hey, boy," muttered Ekion, behind him. "You're taking us the wrong way! That fork back there, it turned south, that's what we want!"

"Only if you fancy a sheer drop of a thousand cubits," said Hylas without turning his head.

Ekion snorted. "So *you* say!"

"Well, yes I do. And just so you know, a bit farther on there's another fork that leads south, but we're not taking that either, as it goes straight round to Lapithos."

The men within earshot sniggered, and Ekion flushed as red as his beard.

There'd been an outcry when Akastos had announced that they'd be following Hylas. A boy not even fifteen, guiding grown men? People had laughed in disbelief, and some had jeered at Hylas, asking where his lion had gone, and what about that girl of his, who could turn herself into a bird?

Ekion was the worst. "That boy's never even *seen* a battle," he'd sneered, "and you're asking us to follow him?"

"I'm not asking," Akastos had replied calmly, "I'm telling."

At that, Ekion had backed down; but ever since, he'd been on the lookout for Hylas to fail.

By mid-afternoon, they'd crested the pass and were

descending into the foothills, when Akastos called a rest halt.

Hylas was beside himself. "Can't they rest when we reach the others?"

"They need food now," said Akastos. "No point getting there if they're too weak to fight."

"No point getting there too late, either," Hylas retorted.

"Hylas. You know the way, I know how to look after my people. Now shut up and eat." Akastos strode off to talk to the scouts who'd been keeping watch for the Crows, and the ragged little army hunkered down among the pines. A woman offered Hylas olives and an acorn cake, but he waved them away and stalked off to find Jinx.

The stallion was at the rear of the column, with the donkeys. All the beasts were being kept as far as possible from Akastos, as they seemed to sense that he was haunted by the Angry Ones, and shied from him in terror.

When Jinx saw Hylas, he whickered a welcome. He seemed calmer and more biddable now that he was part of a herd, and he hadn't even balked at carrying a load of supplies.

"Why can't we keep going?" growled Hylas as he stroked the stallion's bony nose. He had a sudden wild impulse to scramble onto Jinx's back and gallop off to find Pirra and Issi.

Jinx was snorting and flaring his nostrils: He'd spotted something on the crag.

Craning his neck, Hylas saw gray figures peering down

at him. His hand went to his *wedjat* amulet. "It's all right, Jinx," he murmured with more conviction than he felt. "They mean us no harm."

Since they'd entered the pass, he'd seen several ghosts. He guessed they were victims of skirmishes who remained unburied and without the proper rites. He hadn't told anyone about them, that would only cause panic; but it made him feel lonelier than ever. If only Pirra were here. Although if she were, he wouldn't tell her the worst of it: that the ghosts were no longer indistinct and glimpsed only from the corner of his eye. He now saw them as clearly as he saw Akastos, or Periphas.

And there was something else that he dreaded even more. It was the thought that, among them, he might see one who would put a brutal end to two summers of hope: the ghost of his own little sister.

<hr />

They hadn't gone far when a commotion in the rear forced another halt. "What *now*?" muttered Hylas.

Something had panicked the donkeys, and Jinx had broken free from the boy who was leading him and taken refuge in a patch of thistles.

By the time Hylas ran back, the donkeys were just about under control, but Jinx was rearing and lunging inside a ring of men who were only making things worse.

"Let me through," panted Hylas. "Get back, all of you!"

Jinx was terrified. His chestnut coat was dark with sweat and he was trembling all over. This isn't ghosts, thought

Hylas, taking hold of the reins and stroking the stallion's rigid neck.

"Something spooked them," said the boy who'd been leading Jinx. With a shaky finger he pointed at a belt of pines high on a crag. "I can't see nothing up there, but I can feel it!" Like Jinx, he was sweating with fear; so was everyone else.

Hylas shaded his eyes with his palm. He went still. It wasn't possible. It was broad daylight—and yet there, perched on the crag like huge shadowy vultures, were the Angry Ones.

His temples ached and his heart hammered against his ribs as he took in Their long snaky necks, Their raw red eyes churning with the fires of Chaos . . .

Jinx snorted and tugged at the reins. Hylas spoke to him soothingly, but inside he fought a panicky urge to run—it didn't matter where, just get away.

At that moment, he heard giant wings shaken out with a leathery rustle. He watched the spirits of air and darkness wheel off and vanish into the clouds. The weight of dread lifted. People around him breathed again.

"What *was* that?" said Akastos a little later, when Hylas was back at the head of the column.

"Something spooked them," Hylas replied.

"I know that," said Akastos, "but what?" Glancing over his shoulder, he leaned closer. "It didn't feel like ghosts," he said under his breath.

"There *are* ghosts in these mountains," said Hylas. "I've seen them."

The sharp light eyes met his. "But that's not what terrified those beasts and made grown men quake."

"But how is it *possible*?" whispered Hylas. "The Angry Ones only come at night, when it's dark!"

"They're getting stronger," Akastos said grimly. "I've felt it for some time. These days, They bring their darkness with Them. That's how it feels to me."

"But why?"

"Who can say? Perhaps it has something to do with the sacrifices of the Crows."

"Then the sooner we reach the others and Hekabi does that charm, the better!"

"If it works," said Akastos.

"What do you mean, you stopped looking for her?" shouted Hylas. "That's why you *went* to Dentra, to find Issi!"

"And I told you," retorted Pirra, "she wasn't there. It was a false lead, Hylas! The shadow thief is a *boy*!"

"How d'you know if you've never even *seen* him?"

"Because Hekabi says so, and she has no reason to lie!"

Pirra was right, but Hylas refused to accept it. That would mean accepting the fact that Issi hadn't been heard of in two whole summers. It would mean accepting that Issi, in all likelihood, was dead.

He and the others had reached the Lykonian rebels' camp around nightfall. It was on the lowermost roots of Mount Lykas, on a long ridge dotted with olive and tamarisk trees, overlooking the Lykonian plains. A motley array of tents and shelters was strung out across the ridge, and several hundred weary and despairing rebels had fallen on the newcomers with a heartfelt welcome. It was good to exchange food and news around the campfires that no longer had to be hidden from the enemy—whose own fires could now be seen in the distance, across the plain.

Akastos and Periphas had gone to confer with the leaders, and Hylas had found Pirra sitting by a fire outside a small tent at the far side of camp. She and Hekabi had arrived shortly before, with the scouts who'd found them on Dentra. Echo was roosting in a nearby tree, but there was no sign of Havoc. Hekabi was off gathering herbs for her charm against the Angry Ones, having confirmed that They were indeed getting stronger. She had made no promise that her charm would work as well as it had before.

When Hylas had found Pirra, she'd been sharpening her knife on her whetstone. Now she sat down again and went back to her work. "I tried my best," she said in a low voice. "But there is no trace of Issi."

In the firelight, Hylas saw how exhausted she was, with bluish shadows under her eyes. "I'm sorry," he said. "I shouldn't have blown up like that."

She scrutinized her knife, then wiped it on her tunic and thrust it into its sheath. "No, you shouldn't," she said.

He sat down beside her and rested his forearms on his knees. "Where's Havoc?"

"In the hills. I don't think she likes all the people and the dogs." She paused. "Do you want me to go and look for her too?"

"Pirra, I said I'm sorry. It's just . . ." He broke off with a scowl. How could he tell her what it had been like? Hoping against hope that finally, after all this time, the guilt and the anxiety would be over, and he would see Issi again? And then to walk into camp and have it all come crashing down.

He glanced at Pirra's crinkly black hair and her pale, severe face. She'd never had a sister. How could he expect her to understand?

Everything feels different now, thought Pirra, watching the embers collapse and send a flurry of sparks into the night sky.

After days in the mountains, the rebel camp had come as a shock. The smells, the dirt, the noise. Donkeys and sheep; dogs foraging for scraps; children running messages; women cooking, tending the wounded, mending armor, making arrows; men and boys getting ready for battle. Everyone was either Messenian or Lykonian, all of them rough and warlike. And Akastos—*Akastos*—was High Chieftain of Mycenae. It was too much to take in. Pirra felt very Keftian: very foreign and out of place.

Hylas too looked tough and warlike, and so Lykonian,

with that nose that made a straight line with his brow. With a pang, she remembered the hope in his tawny eyes when he'd found her, and how the light had died when she'd told him she hadn't found Issi.

"Have you eaten?" he asked.

"Yes," she lied. "You?"

"Mm."

Their eyes met, and they glanced quickly away. Then of one accord they rose and stood looking at the campfires on the ridge, and all the tired and dirty people. Behind them, Mount Lykas blotted out the stars. On its roots to the north, Pirra made out a clutch of glimmering red pinpricks: Hekabi had told her that that was the Crows' stronghold of Lapithos. East across the plains, the darkness was seamed with a swath of more red sparks.

"That's Pharax's camp," Hylas said quietly.

Pirra swallowed. "There are so many of them."

"There'll be more soon. According to the scouts, Telamon's forces have made it through the main pass, and they're massing to the south."

"Which means we'll be attacked from the south *and* the east."

In the dark, she saw him nod. "Akastos says we'll take up position just below this ridge, not far from camp." He paused. "If the battle goes against us, the women and children must flee to the hills. He says the Crows will reach us late tomorrow. That's when the battle will begin."

"'*We* will take up position'?" she said sharply. "You're not thinking of taking part in the battle?"

He looked down at her. "Of course I am."

"But—Hylas . . . The Crows have the dagger. That means they can't be beaten!"

"Well—but if what we hear is true, and Pharax has it, I might be able to find some way of getting it off him—"

"*How?*" she burst out. "Hylas—Pharax is a grown man and a seasoned fighter! He's the best warrior the Crows have got!"

There was a dangerous silence. "Are you saying I should run away?" he said in a hard voice. "Be a coward, like my father?"

"Of course not! I'm saying that if—if we're to have a hope of beating them, it won't be in battle!"

"Then how?"

"I don't *know*! But—"

"*If the Outsider wields the blade, the House of Koronos burns.* How will I get to 'wield the blade,' Pirra, if I'm not in the battle?"

"But there *must* be another way! The Oracle *can't* mean for you to go into battle: You're not a warrior; you've never even worn armor!"

She'd gone too far. "Nor have quite a lot of these peasants with their sickles," he retorted, "or these fishermen with their spears! Pirra, none of us knows how to fight, not really—apart from Akastos and Periphas and a handful of others—but what else can we do!"

"And what about me?" she flung back. "What am *I* supposed to do? Wait meekly here in camp, and pray they don't bring you back in pieces on a shield? Well I won't do it, Hylas! There has to be another way of fighting the Crows, and I'm going to find it!"

18

"He says a battlefield's no place for a girl," snarled Pirra, pacing up and down in front of Hekabi. "As if we'll be any safer here if the Crows win!"

"But it's Hylas you're worried about," Hekabi said calmly.

"Because he's going to get himself killed! And the stupid thing is, even if he did manage to get the dagger off Pharax, there'd be no *point*! He's not a god, he can't destroy it on his own in the middle of a battle—and I doubt very much that the Lady of the Wild Things is going to come down and do it for him just because he asks Her to!"

Hekabi bent over a steaming pot hanging over the fire. Pirra went on pacing. At one stroke, Hylas had made her feel utterly powerless and sick with dread. "We're missing something," she said. "We're doing this all wrong, why can't he *see* that?"

Hekabi ladled sludge into two wooden bowls and set them on the ground.

"What's that?" said Pirra. "Some sort of spell?"

"Barley gruel. Eat." Taking two horn spoons from her goatskin bag, she stuck one in each bowl.

Irritably, Pirra waved hers away. Then she discovered she was ravenous, and snatched it up. As she wolfed her gruel, she glanced at Hekabi, calmly eating. "You always said there was no hope for him," she said with her mouth full.

"Not quite," mumbled Hekabi. "I said he has a destiny, so his life is not his own."

"You mean the Oracle."

"And the visions. They're part of it too."

Pirra stopped eating and waited for her to go on.

"Hylas told you once," said the wisewoman, "that on Thalakrea, he saw the Lady of Fire. He asked Her to save everyone else and take him instead—and She touched his temple with Her burning finger and said, *I already have.*"

Pirra set down her bowl. "I thought of that too. You think the Lady means to take him, just like She said. You think—you think he's going to die."

"Maybe."

Black spots swam before Pirra's eyes. "You really think there's no hope?"

"For him? Who knows? For the rest of us?" Placing her bowl on the ground, Hekabi spread her hands. "Although we've more of a chance now that Akastos is leader."

Pirra saw the High Chieftain in the distance, at the center of a ring of men. He listened gravely to one, nodded to a second, spoke briefly to a third, then strode off for another part of camp. The men he left behind appeared calmer and more purposeful: He'd given them strength.

"I wasn't all that surprised when I found out who he really is," said Hekabi, watching him. "A great leader has the power to make people believe in themselves. Akastos can do that. Who knows where it'll lead?"

"But what about *Hylas?*" Pirra burst out. "How can you think it's his destiny to go charging into battle and throw away his life?"

"I don't know what his destiny is. Only the gods know that."

"But you're a wisewoman; you're *supposed* to know!"

Hekabi scraped up the last of her gruel and licked her spoon. "While you were arguing with your lion-haired Akean, I did a fire reading, to see how the battle would go."

"And?"

"I heated the blade of a bronze ax till it was red-hot, then I dropped on a handful of pebbles—rock crystal, jasper—and saw how they moved."

"So who will win?" Pirra said impatiently.

"The stones didn't say. But one of them—a crystal—leaped clean off the blade and into the fire."

Pirra gasped. This was almost worse than she'd feared. "You think that's *Hylas?* You think he'll *run away?*"

"I don't know. What I do know is that you can do nothing for him now. You *must* leave him to do what he thinks is right."

Pirra clenched her teeth. "Well, I refuse simply to wait here till it's over! There must be other ways of fighting the Crows!"

Hekabi did not reply. She sat facing Mount Lykas with her hands clasped about her knees. Her expression was thoughtful, but Pirra sensed her fierce intent.

Following the wisewoman's gaze to the mountain's lower slopes, Pirra made out the distant red glimmer of torchlight. That's Lapithos, she thought. The Crows' ancestral stronghold, where they first began all those years ago, before they sought richer lands to the north, and attacked Mycenae itself . . .

An idea came to her, and she caught her breath. It was so outrageous, so impossible . . . "I've just thought of something," she said. "I wonder . . . I wonder if you've had the same idea?"

Hekabi turned her head. Firelight played on the streak of white hair at her temple, and her eyes gleamed. "You tell me."

Pirra licked her lips. "The rebels say the Crows have taken half of everything the peasants produce—and it's all up there in the storerooms at Lapithos. Linen, wool . . . Jar upon jar of olive oil."

Hekabi's lip curled, the closest she ever got to a smile. "They'd better be careful," she said softly. "Someone might start a fire. And you know what the Oracle says: *The House of Koronos burns . . .*"

With a stick, Pirra jabbed the embers. She watched

the flurry of sparks shooting skyward. If the rebels lost tomorrow, then in all likelihood, Hylas would be killed. That was too awful to contemplate. She concentrated on revenge.

"What if the Crows did win the battle," she murmured, "and they made it back to Lapithos, only—"

Hekabi barked a mirthless laugh. "Only to find nothing there but a pile of smoking ruins!"

The eve of battle, and everyone busy: painting shields, mending armor, sharpening weapons. Keeping their minds off tomorrow.

Archers trimmed their beards and tied back their hair so that it wouldn't get in the way. Slingers filled their pouches with the smoothest, roundest pebbles. Every man washed himself, oiled his skin, combed and braided his hair—so that if he was killed the next day, he would be fit to meet his gods.

Akastos had ordered Hylas to get himself kitted out, and the women had given him a quilted linen tunic and a kilt of sturdy pigskin, a hauberk, a ridiculously heavy oxhide shield, and—to his astonishment—a full set of bronze armor.

The tunic was unwieldy and hot, the armor made him feel like a beetle, and the helmet had earflaps that muffled his hearing; he found a quiet place and sat down to cut them off. He was ashamed to find that his hands were shaking uncontrollably; he could hardly hold his knife.

"Here," said Akastos, making him jump. The High Chieftain dropped two leather wrist cuffs into his lap. "They stop the sweat running onto your hands and spoiling your grip."

"Thanks," muttered Hylas, praying that Akastos hadn't noticed him trembling.

To change the subject, he asked where Akastos had gotten his own bronze armor, and his splendid sword with the gold hilt. Akastos replied that it had been his own at Mycenae, and Periphas had hidden it years ago along with his sealstone, when the Crows had taken over. "He was about your age at the time. He never accepted the story that I was dead."

Hylas jammed the helmet on his head and stood up. It was a hot night, and the air felt heavy. He drew a deep breath, but still felt breathless. "What's on your sealstone?" he asked.

Akastos showed him. It was green jasper, carved with a warrior standing beside a lion, with one hand on its mane.

"The Lion of Mycenae," said Hylas. Havoc still hadn't made an appearance, and he missed her savagely.

He asked Akastos if Hekabi had done the charm against the Angry Ones. The High Chieftain nodded slowly. "She gave me this." He touched a small black pouch on a thong around his neck. "But she said we can't be sure it'll work— or for how long."

"Well, it's dark and there's no sign of Them," Hylas said hopefully. "Maybe that's down to the charm."

Akastos' mouth twisted. "Maybe. But whether it works or not, I'll lead the rebels tomorrow. I have to. Tomorrow either we crush the Crows, or they crush us." He spoke calmly, and he looked immensely strong and capable: an experienced warrior who'd fought many battles.

What am I *doing* here? Hylas thought suddenly. Pirra's right. I'm a boy among men, I'm not up to this.

The High Chieftain gave him a searching glance, then jerked his head. "Come with me."

They walked to the edge of camp, where the sounds of voices and pack animals gave way to the throbbing ring of night crickets.

Akastos pointed south, to a stretch of rocky ground. "You can't see it from here, but there's a gully that'll stop Telamon's forces attacking from that side, so he'll have to move round and join forces with Pharax. Which means that they'll all be facing west—and by the time the battle begins—"

Hylas caught his breath. "The Sun will be in their eyes!"

Akastos nodded.

"That's clever. But—we'll still be massively outnumbered. And yet you sound as if you think we might win."

"There's always hope." Akastos fell silent. Then he said in an altered voice: "Hylas, I need to know something. When we were in the pass, you said you'd seen ghosts. Were they—did you see one who looked like me, only younger?"

Hylas shook his head. "I'm sorry. If your brother's ghost was there, I didn't see him."

Akastos nodded sadly, and his gaze turned inward, into the past. Hylas couldn't tell if he feared to see his brother's ghost, or longed to.

Mustering his courage, Hylas asked the question he'd wanted to ask since last winter. "How—why did you kill him?"

Akastos blew out a long breath. "A woman. He was in love with her, and the Crows told him that I wanted her too. They said she refused me, and I forced her. So my brother, he picked a fight with me . . ." He glanced down at his hand resting on the hilt of his sword. "Tomorrow's my last chance, Flea. Fifteen years ago, I swore to crush the Crows and appease my brother's ghost. If I can kill Pharax, or Telamon—if I can shed the lifeblood of a highborn Crow—my brother's ghost will be at peace. And I will be rid of the Angry Ones forever."

He spoke as if he truly believed he could do it, and Hylas felt a surge of love for this man who'd endured years of unimaginable hardship and terror, and yet had never given up.

But Akastos was also a warrior who knew what to do in battle, and as Hylas stared across the plains at the distant campfires of the Crows, he thought of all the swords and daggers and arrows that tomorrow would be aimed at him. He wished passionately that he were a woman or a child, and could stay behind in camp.

"You're scared," Akastos said softly.

He nodded. "Does that make me a coward, like my

father? Will I do what he did, and run away from battle?"

"There's something you should know about your father, Flea. When Ekion captured you, you told him that that tattoo on your arm was Mountain Clan: your father's clan. And once, on Keftiu, you said that your mother left you and your sister on the mountain, wrapped in a bearskin." He paused. "That told me something. It told me that your father wasn't just some member of the Mountain Clan. He was their leader."

Hylas blinked.

"He refused to fight because he thought his people would have a better chance if they took to the mountains."

"Because he was a coward!" Hylas said hotly.

"He did what he thought was right for his people." Again he paused. "And when the Crows finally hunted him down, he fought to the end, and he made a good death."

"But he didn't fight when you needed him," Hylas said stubbornly.

"No. No, he didn't."

"Well, I will."

"I know you will, Flea." He put his hand on Hylas' shoulder. "Every man is frightened before a battle."

"Even you?"

"Oh, yes. The more battles you fight, the harder it gets."

Hylas opened his mouth to reply, but at that moment, Nomios ran up with a question for Akastos and they went off together, leaving Hylas on his own.

He found a lonely tamarisk tree and made an offering of

half his rations to the Lady of the Wild Things, asking Her to keep Pirra, Havoc, and Echo safe, and Issi, wherever she was—and to let Akastos and Periphas survive the battle—"and me too, if possible, but above all, the others." Then he went in search of Pirra.

He found the tent she shared with Hekabi empty, and all their belongings gone.

"They left," said a woman mending a tunic nearby.

"Where'd they go?"

The woman bit off a thread and waved an arm vaguely at the mountain. "Dunno why."

Hylas stood staring into the darkness, with the hot wind stinging his eyes.

There has to be another way of fighting the Crows, Pirra had cried. *And I'm going to find it!*

And now she was gone, and he had no idea where, or why. All he knew was that he might never see her again.

Ten paces away among the thorn bushes, he made out a large gray shape. "Havoc!" he whispered.

Havoc's eyes threw back the starlight as she raised her muzzle and snuffed his scent; but instead of bounding toward him, she turned and melted silently into the shadows.

First Pirra, and now Havoc.

Hylas glanced back at camp, where people were rolling themselves in cloaks and settling to sleep. So many people . . .

And yet he'd never felt so alone.

19

Once again, the boy called to the she-lion. He needed her, she could hear it in his voice. She longed to burst from her hiding place and bound down to him, to fling her forepaws around his neck and give him a good muzzle-rub.

And yet—the little half-grown human needed her too. The little human was miserable up there on the mountain, and she was far too young to be by herself.

Kneading the dust with her claws, the she-lion wondered what to do. The hot wind carried a tangle of scents from the vast human lair spread out below: She smelled goats, dogs, donkeys, even a horse—and so many people. She had an idea that the girl and the falcon were among them, although it had been a while since she'd caught their scents. Surely with them to comfort him, the boy couldn't be lonely for long?

A dog barked angrily. Then another and another. It sounded as if they'd caught the she-lion's scent, and were warning her to keep out. She twitched her tail in scorn. What did they think, that she could be frightened off by a pack of *dogs*?

She hunkered down and watched the boy pacing up and down, unable to tear herself away.

After a while, the dark-maned human who was the leader came back again. He spoke quietly to the boy. The boy shook his head and pointed at the bushes where the she-lion was hiding, and she knew that although he couldn't see her, he sensed that she was still there.

Should she go to him? Or should she seek the little half-grown human who so badly needed looking after? It hurt to see the boy so miserable. But he was safe here among his kind, and he had the girl and the falcon and the dark-maned human. The little one on the mountain had no one.

This little human puzzled the she-lion a lot, because she smelled so very like the boy. She had the same tawny eyes as him, the same lion-colored mane, the same laugh; she even played the same game with a ball of sticks. She *had* to be of the same pride; the she-lion felt this in her fur. And if that was true, the she-lion had to protect her, just as she'd protected the girl and the falcon.

Besides, she *liked* the little human, who was tough and extremely good at hiding. For a long time she'd cleverly masked her scent, by smearing herself in mud and wrapping her head in fish skins. She was also an absolutely brilliant climber, and could scramble up trees much better than the she-lion.

The she-lion hesitated, while the scents flowed down to her from the mountain: pines, a night heron, a stag. It was *such* a good mountain, with so much prey and not too many lions. It would make an excellent range for the pride; surely even the falcon would think so?

But it was no place for a little human cub on her own.

The she-lion thought of the male lion who'd stalked the girl a few Darks ago. That young lion wasn't experienced enough to catch big prey by himself—so for him, a little human cub would be an easy kill.

The she-lion vividly remembered when she herself had been a tiny weak cub, and the evil crow-men had killed her mother and father. For a few dreadful Lights and Darks, she'd been on her own. She'd never forgotten the hunger and the terror of the buzzards swooping down to attack. It had been awful—until the boy had found her and made everything better.

For the last time, the boy called to her.

The she-lion gave a low, anguished mew. But she didn't stir from her hiding place.

Wistfully, she watched him trudge back toward the lair with the dark-maned human. Then she turned and headed up the mountain. She knew now what she had to do: She must find the little human cub and keep her safe. Then she must think of some way for them all to be together: herself, the boy, the girl, the falcon, and the little human.

Yes. The pride must be together, in their beautiful new range. This was how things should be.

20

Telamon had been feeling much better since he'd resolved to seize the dagger from his grandfather. The terror of the Angry Ones had faded, and not even the thought of his father's ghost could trouble him now.

True, not all was going to plan, for his men had failed to catch Hylas. *But victory comes to he who dares,* he told himself as he cantered up the track toward Lapithos. *Once I have the dagger, no Outsider shall stand in my way.*

Earlier, he'd left Ilarkos in command of his men, with orders to lead them through the pass and down on to the plains, where they would make contact with Pharax and the main force.

Ilarkos had been alarmed. "But my lord, what will I tell the lord Pharax if he asks where you are?"

"You won't need to tell him anything; by then I'll have caught up with you, or seen him myself." With that, Telamon had slapped the reins on his horse's neck and started for the stronghold where he'd grown up.

As the Sun rose higher, he saw charcoal stormclouds massing in the east, and for a moment, the thought of

Pharax cast a shadow over his spirit. Telamon remembered the night he'd returned from Egypt, when his uncle had interrogated him in the great hall at Mycenae. Not a muscle had moved in Pharax's gaunt countenance as Telamon had told of Alekto's dreadful death. And afterward, Pharax hadn't mentioned her once, he'd merely demanded to know why Telamon had disobeyed his orders by becoming involved in a skirmish on the Great River. Pharax didn't *care* that his own sister had been eaten by crocodiles—but if his orders were flouted, he would not forgive.

Well, and what of that? thought Telamon rebelliously. Only the bravest of men would dare disobey Pharax—and *I* am that man. When I've seized the dagger from Koronos, then Pharax will have to obey *me*.

He saw himself driving his chariot at the head of his warriors, brandishing the dagger aloft and sending the last of the rebels fleeing in panic. Already he could feel its weight in his hand, its strength coursing through him. He saw its strong clean lines and the lethal sweep of its blade; the quartered circle on its hilt that signified a chariot wheel to crush his enemies.

The first-ever chieftain of the House of Koronos, the warrior who'd built his stronghold at Lapithos, had forged the dagger from the helmet of his slaughtered enemy, and had quenched its burning bronze with blood from his own battle wounds. With ancestors like that, was it any wonder that the gods had decreed that Telamon should rule?

At last Lapithos rose into sight, and his heart swelled with pride. It sat with its back against the mountain, dominating all it surveyed. Crows wheeled and cawed above its dark red walls, and on the watchtowers that squatted at each corner, the black crests of the guards' helmets streamed in the wind.

Reining in his horse, Telamon turned and stared down over the rich plains of Lykonia, with their olive groves and barley fields stretching all the way to the mountains of the east. Below and much nearer, he saw the ant-like rebels clustered on their ridge. There were more of them than he'd expected; but not enough to withstand the great red dust cloud on the plain that was Pharax's forces. It was still some distance away, but moving inexorably closer.

With a thrill of pride, Telamon pictured the glory he would win in battle. We will crush them to the last man, he thought. We will enslave their women and children. That rabble down there will be no match for the House of Koronos.

The sentries on the walls had seen him, and the great bronze-studded gates creaked open to let him in. Clattering into the courtyard, he leaped off his horse and flung the reins to a slave.

The captain of the guard hurried toward him, bowing. From the man's babbled greeting, Telamon grasped that the guards were beginning to lose their nerve, after watching the rebels massing on the ridge.

"More of 'em than we thought, my lord," the captain said apprehensively. "And the omens are bad—"

"What omens," growled Telamon, snatching a wine cup from a slave girl and draining it.

"Starlings, my lord, a great cloud of 'em, never seen so many! Flew right over us, darkened the sky. They even scared the crows off for a time. And that's not all, my lord, there are rumors—"

"What rumors?" snapped Telamon. "Go on man, spit it out!"

"My lord, they say . . ." He gulped. "They say that the Lion of Mycenae has returned."

Silence in the courtyard: Every man was watching to see how Telamon took that. He noticed that most of them were very young, some still without beards. It appeared that Pharax had taken the experienced warriors, and left Koronos guarded by boys.

This made Telamon feel manly and in control. "The 'Lion of Mycenae,'" he said in a scornful voice that rang across the courtyard, "is merely a name that cowardly peasants once gave to a man called Akastos, whom my grandfather killed a long time ago, when he seized control of Mycenae. Such tales are for women, not warriors." His glance raked the guards, who hung their heads in shame. "If I hear any more gossip like that, I'll have you all flogged!"

Flinging down the wine cup, he turned to the captain. "You've wasted enough of my time," he barked. "Take me to High Chieftain Koronos, I must speak with him at once!"

It still gave Telamon a shock to enter the great hall of Lapithos, and find Koronos there instead of Thestor, his father.

Koronos sat at the far end, on a bench behind a richly carved table of gilded wood. He was alone, except for the guards at the doorway and a slave who was mixing wine with honey and crumbled cheese in a great silver bowl. The slave looked frightened. So did the guards. Everyone was frightened of Koronos. Fear surrounded him like a mist.

Telamon strode past the great central hearth where the fire had been burning for generations. He passed the throne of green marble against the west wall: the throne that had been Thestor's. His heart skipped a beat. For an instant, from the corner of his eye, he glimpsed his father's ghost, watching him with grim disapproval.

Very deliberately, Telamon turned his head and stared at the throne. It was empty, of course. *Lies, lies,* he told himself, with a surge of hatred at Hylas for planting fears in his mind and making him see things that weren't there. Then all that was forgotten, and he was striding toward the High Chieftain.

"Koronos," he said brusquely, dropping to one knee and putting his hand to his heart.

His grandfather regarded him in silence.

As always, Koronos wore the purple tunic and white goatskin mantle of the High Chieftain of Mycenae, secured at the shoulder by a gold cloak pin the size of a clenched fist. A spiked circlet of hammered gold bound his temples, and around his waist was the great golden belt of the House of Koronos, with its clasp in the form of four axes radiating like a jagged star. Age had silvered the High Chieftain's beard and scraped the hair from his skull, but instead of draining him of strength, it had turned him to granite.

Telamon had always been terrified of him—but now, as he rose to his feet, he noticed the iron ring on his grandfather's thumb. There had been a time when Koronos had only worn that ring for important sacrifices, but these days, he was never without it. Did this mean that even Koronos was afraid of the Angry Ones?

Telamon found this oddly heartening. His grandfather was not invincible after all.

"Why are you not with your men," said the High Chieftain in the voice that made seasoned warriors turn pale.

Telamon took a deep breath. *Courage,* he told himself. "I don't have much time," he said harshly. "Soon the battle will begin and I must be there." He squared his shoulders. "I've come for the dagger. I need it to lead our men to victory."

Silence in the hall. The old man licked his lipless mouth with a slow, pale tongue. *"You?"* he said drily.

Telamon caught a lethal glint in the hooded eyes. He clenched his jaw. "The men need to see it, Koronos. It's doing no good hidden away up here."

With appalling deliberation, Koronos rose to his full height. "When I'm dead, you can fight Pharax for the dagger. While I live, *boy*, you will obey me."

Telamon flinched. Then he lifted his chin. "Listen to me!" he spat. "I am young, Koronos—and you are *old*! Soon, you will die."

The slave gasped and fled the hall in terror of his master's wrath. But Koronos' features never moved.

"You will give me the dagger," said Telamon, meeting his grandfather's stare.

A harsh bark of laughter rang through the hall, making Telamon step back. Over his shoulder, he saw the guards at the doorway exchange startled glances: Like him, they'd never heard the High Chieftain laugh.

"I sent it to Pharax days ago," Koronos replied. "I want a *man* to take it into battle—not a boy."

Telamon felt the blood drain from his cheeks. *Pharax has the dagger*, he thought in disbelief. *You've come all this way for nothing.*

Numbly, he watched his grandfather resume his seat and place one granite fist on the table. "Your father was weak," Koronos said coldly. "He tried to keep himself and his son apart from his clan: He had no stomach to rule. You are weak too. Despite your bluster, you are *afraid*. Now get out of my sight. And try not to disgrace yourself on the battlefield."

There was a roaring in Telamon's ears. A red mist came down over his eyes. He pictured himself thrusting his sword through his grandfather's mottled throat . . . blood bubbling and frothing from that lipless mouth . . .

With an immense effort of will, he turned on his heel and staggered down the hall, with Koronos' stony laughter ringing in his ears.

21

Wheezing with laughter, Issi threw herself out of the chestnut tree and landed in the water lilies with a satisfying splash.

Havoc leaped in after her with an even bigger splash, swamping the riverbank. Issi swam under the lioness' belly and made a grab at her tail, but Havoc twisted around and ducked beneath *her,* eliciting bubbly underwater squeals. Still play-fighting, they burst out together in a spluttering spray.

Breathless and spent, Issi scrambled onto a rock, and Havoc did the same, shaking the water from her fur and slumping down beside her.

It was a hot night, pulsing with the voices of crickets and frogs. Issi lay on her back, gazing at the Moon between the chestnut tree's branches. She still couldn't believe how quickly things had changed. A while ago, she'd been sitting under this tree with her head in her hands, so lonely and miserable that she couldn't summon the will to move. Then Havoc had come bounding out of the reeds, rubbing against her and making happy little groany *owmp owmp* noises.

Putting out her hand, Issi touched the lioness' rough, leathery pad. *Thank you for coming to find me,* she told Havoc silently.

She must have slept, because when she opened her eyes, the night was turning gray, and Havoc was back from a hunt, hauling a dead buck by its neck over the ground.

Once, Issi had seen a pride of lions feeding on a boar. She'd felt a twinge of envy as she'd watched the orderly little family at its meal: the male lion eating first, followed by the lionesses, and then the cubs. They'd been so at ease with each other, so close. Issi had never known her own parents. Hylas had been the only family she'd ever had.

Pushing that thought away, Issi woke up a fire and waited respectfully for Havoc to eat her fill. After a while, she was rewarded with an affectionate nudge from the lioness' big, bloody muzzle: *Go on, it's your turn.*

Issi hacked chunks of venison and set them to roast, then cracked the thighbones and guzzled the delicious, fatty marrow. After this she got fed up with waiting, and gobbled the meat half raw, till she was as full and filthy as Havoc. She gave a contented burp. It felt so *good* to be part of a pride.

Sparrows chattered in the chestnut tree, and a thrush began its morning song. The forest was waking up. In the strengthening light, Issi watched Havoc's pelt turn from its nighttime silver to daytime tawny. She loved the lioness' enormous paws and the leathery smell of her pads, she loved the deep black fur inside her ears. Most of all, she loved Havoc's huge, slanted, dark-rimmed eyes of that beautiful red-gold, like sunlight through autumn leaves.

Thank you for coming to find me, Issi told her again.

Havoc hauled herself to her feet and waded into the shallows to lap the water. Then she ambled over to the chestnut tree, rose on her hind legs, and started scratching deep grooves in its trunk. As she flexed her claws in and out, her muscles rippled beneath her pelt, and she slitted her eyes with pleasure.

Issi knew better than to disturb her, so she scrambled up the other side of the trunk, picked a handful of chestnuts, and sat on a branch with her legs dangling, splitting open the prickly fruit and munching the nuts. She wondered what Hylas was doing now. With a stab of jealousy, she wondered if Pirra had found him, and they were together again.

On her way down the tree, she came upon one of Havoc's claw-sheaths embedded in the bark, like a fingernail. This pleased Issi immensely: It was almost as good as an actual claw, and it felt like an excellent omen. With a flake of flint, she drilled a hole in the claw sheath, then made a string from nettle stems and hung the sheath around her neck. There: The best, most powerful amulet she could ever have. This *had* to be a good sign.

The Sun rose higher and the heat intensified. The crickets' song grew louder and faster, and the birds lapsed into stunned silence. Issi felt the slight pressure behind her ears that told her a storm was coming.

Havoc lay on her side, rumbling in her sleep. Issi snuggled against her and dozed, luxuriating in the amazing, unfamiliar feeling of being utterly safe.

Drowsily, she chided herself for having been so miserable. So *what* if Hylas was friends with that girl? Maybe they would have a fight, and Pirra would go back to Keftiu and never bother them again. Issi didn't want anything *bad* to happen to her; she just wanted to be with Hylas, the way it used to be, with no one in the way.

But all that was a problem for the future. The main thing was to *find* him. And with Havoc to guide her, surely that would only be a matter of time?

To Issi's surprise, Havoc woke well before noon. The lioness seemed alert and keen to be off, uttering eager little whines as she snuffed the air. It looked as if she'd caught an exciting scent. *Could it be Hylas?*

Certainly, the lioness seemed very sure of where she was going, skirting the mountainside at a brisk trot that had Issi struggling to keep up. But whenever she dropped too far behind, Havoc paused and waited for her, which strengthened Issi's belief that Havoc might be leading her to her brother.

The morning grew even hotter and more airless. To the east, Issi saw grape-colored clouds. She heard the crazy laughter of a green woodpecker. She noticed that the swallows were flying lower than usual, and the bees were staying close to their nests. *Definitely a storm on the way,* she thought. But she wasn't worried; she was used to storms, and Havoc was keeping to the mountain's lower slopes, where there were caves for shelter—so there'd be little danger from the lightning that stalked the peaks.

Havoc stood halfway up the slope, waiting for her. The lioness blended so perfectly with the long gold grass that it was hard even for Issi to make her out.

As Issi drew near, Havoc turned northeast, toward a spur that jutted from the mountain's roots. Issi hesitated. *Not that way, Havoc, that leads to Lapithos!*

But Havoc had picked up her pace, as if she was nearing her goal. Warily, Issi followed, keeping to the long grass and the tall purple sword-thistles.

As she climbed higher, the view opened up, and she saw the rebels' camp down on the ridge. To the east, on the plain, she saw a vast swath of red dust moving toward them like a tide. Her belly turned over. That must be the Crows. When they reached the rebels, the battle would begin. By the look of it, that would be today.

Havoc had vanished into the grass. Hurrying after her, Issi's heart began to race. What if she found Hylas on the other side of this spur?

As she reached its crest, she heard someone not far below: Someone who, like her, seemed to be heading for Lapithos. Whipping out her knife, she dropped to a crouch. If it was Crows . . .

A clump of thistles blocked her view, she couldn't see who was coming; but on the other side of the spur, she saw Lapithos. With a twinge of fear, she took in its dark red walls, its watchtowers with their slitted windows like sleepless eyes. She saw the fluttering crests of the guards' helmets on top of the walls. The gates stood slightly open: At any moment, Crow warriors might come pouring out of them—or were the gates about to be flung wide to admit whoever was coming?

They were drawing closer; she could hear the grass rustling not ten paces away. It didn't sound like Crows: She caught no creak of armor. Her heart thudded in her chest. *Could* it be Hylas?

The disappointment was so crushing, she felt as if she'd been punched. It wasn't Hylas she saw moving swiftly yet stealthily toward Lapithos.

It was the wisewoman and Pirra.

22

A gust of wind shivered the long grass and blew dust in Pirra's eyes. Her head was swimming with fatigue after climbing into the hills for most of the night, and sweat was trickling down her sides. She tried to ignore the purple stormclouds rolling in from the east, and the tide of red dust slowly advancing across the plain toward the rebel camp. Soon the battle would begin, and Hylas would be in it.

"So that's Lapithos," murmured Hekabi, peering at the Crows' ancestral stronghold, fifty paces ahead. "As I thought. Only a few guards left."

Pirra didn't reply. Lapithos was much smaller and cruder than the House of the Goddess where she'd grown up, but far more warlike and intimidating. She thought it resembled a monstrous toad squatting on the roots of the mountain. Flocks of crows wheeled above it, and vultures glided on huge, fingered wings. Atop the oxblood walls, she saw helmets with crests streaming in the wind. She pictured the guards with bows and arrows poised to shoot.

The idea of setting fire to this impenetrable stronghold—which had seemed so recklessly inviting when they were safe in the rebel camp—now struck her as suicidal folly.

"Hekabi, this is madness," she hissed. "The whole place is bristling with Crows!"

"Then why," breathed the wisewoman, "was Havoc so relaxed when she passed us just now? And look at Echo!"

She was right. Earlier, they'd glimpsed Havoc on the spur, moving calmly through the long grass. As for Echo, having regained her strength, she was having a marvelous time, soaring almost out of sight, then hurtling out of the Sun in one of her astonishing dives, and scattering the crows above the stronghold.

"But even if you're right," whispered Pirra, "there's no way we can get in without being seen!"

Hekabi was peering intently at the helmets on the walls. "Yes there is. Those gates are ajar. I say we just walk straight in."

Pirra shot her a horrified glance. But Hekabi was already striding fearlessly toward the vast double gates that fronted the stronghold.

Muttering a quick prayer to the Goddess, Pirra followed, keeping low and darting from one thorn bush to the next.

To her amazement, no shouts came from above, no hiss of arrows. A shadow sped over her and she ducked—but it was only Echo, heading for the gates. Drawing in her wings at the last moment, the falcon shot through the narrow gap between them.

They were massively thick and studded with bronze, mounted on posts hewn from whole pines. "This *has* to be a trap!" muttered Pirra.

Hekabi pushed them wider and went inside. Nothing happened. Pirra went after her with her heart in her mouth.

She found herself in a courtyard with doorways on all sides. From one, she heard a donkey bray and the snort and stamp of horses. From another, smoke wafted: She guessed that was a cookhouse; she caught the mouthwatering smell of roast pork. In a corner of the courtyard shaded by a gnarled and ancient vine, vultures squabbled over the remains of a meal on a rough table that had been abandoned in a hurry. Between the heaving wings and snaky necks, Pirra saw broken flatbreads, goats' cheese, salted fish, a dripping jar of barley beer.

She was wondering what all this meant when a gust of wind sent the dust whirling across the courtyard and she caught movement on the watchtower. "Hekabi, watch out!" she cried.

But the arrows she dreaded didn't come. Instead, a helmet came crashing down from above and rolled to rest on the stones.

"See?" said Hekabi with a curl of her lip. "There's nobody here!"

Echo shot out of a doorway and swooped in to land on Pirra's shoulder. The feathers beneath the falcon's chin were fluffed up: She was excited, but not alarmed.

"I knew it!" cried Hekabi. "There's nobody *in* those

helmets up there! They left them on the walls to make it look like it's guarded, but they've all *gone*! Lapithos is deserted, Pirra! This is going to work!"

—————

"We still don't know for sure that there's nobody here," breathed Pirra.

"Then we'll have to work fast," retorted Hekabi.

There were two lines of storerooms, one on the east side of the courtyard and one on the west. "We'll start in the east," said Hekabi. "One of the scouts told me that's where most of the oil is. It'll catch fire quicker."

The first storeroom they reached was packed with man-high jars of wine and oil, and big bales of linen and wool. Pirra tried to ignore the panicky feeling she always got in cramped spaces, and did as Hekabi was doing, fetching straw from the stables and hastily twisting it into sheaves, then sticking them in the jars, to act as giant wicks.

Somewhere, a door banged and a horse whinnied. Pirra froze. "There's someone here, I can feel it!" At any moment she expected running feet and the creak of rawhide armor. "Why would they all leave, Hekabi? Why?"

"Who knows?" snapped the wisewoman. "Maybe they went to join the battle, maybe the ones who were left took fright and fled!" With glittering eyes, she unraveled a bale of wool and strewed it about, so that it would burn more easily. "I counted four more storerooms on this side," she said over her shoulder. "I'll do the rest here, you take the ones across the courtyard, and we'll meet outside on the spur—"

"But surely a single room will be enough? Let's just set fire to this one and get *out* of here!"

"No, we have to be *sure*! These roofbeams are hard as stone. For the whole place to go up in smoke, we'll need the strongest, hottest fire, or it'll simply burn out!"

After a brief, fierce dispute, which Hekabi won, Pirra stomped off across the courtyard clutching more straw.

The stone passageway felt cold, and in the cramped space, her breath was unpleasantly loud. She smelled rank sweat: Men had passed here, and not long ago.

Suddenly, she was gripped by an appalling feeling of being trapped. For an instant, she couldn't see, she couldn't move: It was as if her arms were pinioned to her sides. Then the feeling was gone as swiftly as it had come. *Echo,* she thought in horror. *Something's happened to Echo.*

At that moment, a shriek rent the air. Then another and another.

Flinging down the straw, Pirra raced up the passage. Echo's shrieks grew louder—then abruptly cut off. *Oh no, no . . .*

Pirra caught a glimmer of light. She burst into a large hall, dimly lit at the far end by a smoldering brazier. In a heartbeat, she took in roofbeams blackened by smoke; a dizzying red-and-green floor; walls daubed with savage pictures of warriors and hunting dogs; and a green marble throne on one side, flanked by two painted lions. In the middle of the hall, a mound of ash in a huge round hearth was guarded by four massive pillars zigzagged in yellow and black.

Pirra sensed that Echo was in here, although she couldn't see where. At her feet lay a cloak and a spear, as if discarded in haste by some guard—but the hall itself was empty.

No it wasn't. At the far end, near the brazier, a man was slumped head down on a gilded table. Pirra couldn't see his face, but she saw his purple tunic and the white goatskin mantle of the High Chieftain of Mycenae. She saw his stony scalp and the gold diadem around his temples, the cloak pin the size of a fist at his shoulder.

She couldn't believe what she was seeing. She had to make sure. Reluctantly, she drew closer. She caught the reek of charcoal from the brazier. She halted.

Koronos lay with his face in a great silver dish of wine. One hand dangled beside him, the other was on the table. Pirra saw its waxen fingers and black nails frozen in the act of clawing at the bowl. She met the dull glare of one lifeless eye.

She wished she had an amulet to ward off Koronos' angry ghost: Without the proper rites, it could not be far away. If Hylas was here, he would have seen it.

Then she heard the scratch of talons on wood. "Echo?" she whispered.

There: in the corner behind Koronos' corpse. Pirra's heart stood still. Someone had bound the falcon's wings to her sides with a strip of cloth, and tied another around her beak and across her eyes; then they'd secured her by her feet to a stool, which they'd set in the shadows. Echo was still breathing, although clearly half dead with fright.

It was then, with an odd sensation of calm, that Pirra realized Hekabi had gotten it wrong: There *was* someone left in Lapithos—and now he had caught her in his trap, using Echo for bait.

Lifting her chin defiantly, Pirra walked past Koronos' corpse, toward Echo. "It's all right, Echo," she said with a catch in her voice. "I'm here. And I'm going to set you free."

"I wouldn't be too sure about that," said Telamon, stepping out from the dark.

23

"Let the falcon go," said Pirra. "It's me you want."

Telamon stared at her in disbelief. She was huddled at his feet with her ankles bound, her arms pinioned behind her back, and a large bruise ripening on her cheek—and yet she was barking orders at him as if he were a peasant.

He'd always known she was brave. Just now, she'd walked fearlessly past his grandfather's body—while he, Telamon, was still reeling from the shock of what had so recently happened.

I never touched him, Telamon told himself. *The gods did it for me. Just as they gave me the idea to search his chambers, in case he'd lied about sending the dagger to Pharax. The gods* kept *me here, so that I could capture Pirra.*

All this flashed through his mind as he stared down at her. Then he said quietly: "Who do you think you are, to give me orders? Do you think you're still the daughter of the High Priestess of Keftiu?"

"I'll always be that."

"You're *nothing*!" he shouted. "You're in *my power*! See

this?" He tapped the scar on his forehead. "Remember Egypt? That bird of yours striking me with its talons? You're lucky I didn't kill it outright! Shall I do it now, eh? Snap its neck between my fingers?"

"No no please—don't touch her!"

"Ah, that's better. You need to beg more, Pirra. It's what women should do."

Turning his back on her, he strolled down the hall and took his place on Thestor's throne—no, *his* throne.

It's true, he thought in amazement, and at last it began to sink in. *With Koronos gone, all this belongs to me.*

At the end of the hall, Pirra was struggling with her bonds. She'd gone clammy and pale, clearly trying not to panic.

"You can't bear being tied up, can you?" he called. "I remember that. It's your worst nightmare, isn't it? Being tied up forever. Well there's no one to help you now."

"Or you," she shot back. "You're all alone, Telamon. Did you know that Lapithos is deserted? That all your men have fled?"

"Callow youths, I'm better off without them! Now why don't you tell me what you're doing here, and where's Hylas?"

She hesitated. "He's here in Lapithos. Very soon, you're going to feel his knife in your guts."

Drawing his sword, he slashed at the shadows. Then he realized his mistake. "Your filthy Keftian tricks can't fool me! If Hylas was really here, he wouldn't have stood by and let me hit you. So I'll ask you again, and if you don't want me to rip your bird's head off, you'll tell me the truth. Where is he?"

"He's on the battlefield," she said quickly. "Fighting alongside the High Chieftain—the *real* one. Oh yes, it's true," she added. "I've seen Akastos myself. The Lion of Mycenae has returned, and the rebels are flocking to his call!"

"Much good will it do them," he flung back; although inside, he was deeply shaken. "Have you forgotten that we have the dagger? That we can't be beaten!"

"Pharax has the dagger, not you."

"But I can take it whenever I want."

"*You*? Take it from Pharax?"

"The gods mean me to have it, not him!" He ran to loom over her, making her flinch. "I should kill you now and have done with it," he panted, "but I don't think I will. You're my reward for after the battle. Now I'll ask you again: What were you doing here?"

She stared up at him with those fathomless dark eyes. "Pharax will never give you the dagger."

"Why do you go on about Pharax?" he yelled. "Pharax is an obstacle, nothing more! Koronos is dead, the gods have chosen *me* to rule!"

"Did you kill Koronos too?"

"I never touched him," he snarled. "I didn't need to; the gods did it for me!"

As if he were watching it happen all over again, Telamon

saw himself staggering down the hall with Koronos' laughter ringing in his ears. He heard that laughter break off in a choking cry. He turned to see Koronos clutching his arm and gaping like a fish. He seemed to be having a seizure. There was something weirdly wrong with one side of his face: eye, cheek, and mouth sagging grotesquely, as if dragged down by the unseen finger of a god.

The guards had run to help, but Telamon had ordered them back. "No one touch him! The gods have struck him down: We must not interfere!"

In fascination, he'd watched his grandfather topple forward with his face in the silver bowl of wine. A dreadful bubbling gurgle, one hand clawing ineffectually at the bowl . . . The massive shoulders shuddered as Koronos began to drown. Then the black fingernails twitched—and went still.

Telamon had stood there a long time, while word had spread and the last of the guards had fled Lapithos in terror.

Finally, he'd summoned the will to approach the corpse. He'd taken it by the shoulders and yanked it upright. Its head had lolled back, and he'd stared down at the slack, wine-stained ruin of an old man's face.

Why was I so terrified of him? he'd wondered.

He'd unfastened the belt from the corpse and let the body fall forward into the wine. He'd fastened the belt about his own waist, and felt instantly stronger and braver. *The High Chieftain is dead: Long live the High Chieftain.*

Turning, he'd scanned the walls, where his painted Ancestors hunted and slaughtered their enemies. *All those years,* he'd thought, *when I feared I'd never be as brave as them . . . But the truth is, I will surpass them! I will be greater than any of them!*

Pirra's sharp voice pierced his dreams. "If it's all the will of the gods, why are you so frightened of the Angry Ones?"

"I'm not frightened," he muttered.

"But you are, I can see it. Pacing up and down, twisting that iron ring of yours. Hylas told me about that. And Koronos has another; are you going to take that too?" Her lip curled with scorn. "You can collect as many rings as you like, Telamon, but you'll never have enough. I think you'll be afraid for the rest of your life!"

"I'm not afraid!" roared Telamon.

His voice echoed around the great hall—and from the walls, his painted Ancestors stared back at him.

He gave a startled laugh. He passed a hand over his face. An idea had come to him of such brilliance that it could only have been sent by a god. "I'm not afraid," he repeated in wonder. "I *know* what to do!"

Now Pirra was the one who was alarmed. She'd gone white to the lips, and her skin glistened with sweat. "What do you mean? What are you going to do?"

"At one stroke," Telamon said to himself, "I will make the dagger safe for*ever.* Yes, that's it! The gods will help me take it from Pharax on the battlefield—and then I'll give it to my Ancestors, and *they* will keep it safe for all eternity!"

And that way, he continued in his head, *the Ancestors will finally be appeased—my father, and Alekto, and Koronos . . . And the Angry Ones will leave me in peace.*

"Where are you going?" Pirra shouted after him as he strode off down the hall.

"To the battle, of course!"

"What about me and Echo?"

He laughed. "You'd better get used to being tied up," he called, "because you're going to stay like that for a while! And when I've won the battle, and the dagger is safe with my Ancestors forever—when I've crushed the rebels and fed Hylas' still-beating heart to the dogs—you're going to spend the rest of your life here at Lapithos, shut up in the women's chambers. Although maybe—if you beg *very* hard—I might let you have one glimpse of the sky, perhaps every other year!"

Hylas glanced behind him at the quiet, forested hills, and thought of Pirra and Havoc and Echo—and maybe Issi too—up there somewhere, safe from all this. Then he turned back to the battlefield, rearranged his grip on his sword, and waited for the order to fight.

He hadn't expected the start of the battle to be so silent and so orderly. Periphas had formed the rebels into lines just in front of the ridge, and positioned the archers and the slingers at the back, ready to shoot over the others' heads, when the Crows advanced within range.

That won't be long now, thought Hylas in the front line. He watched the vast Crow army marching toward them in clouds of red dust. It was almost within arrowshot. He could hear the creak of armor and the clink of weapons. He could *see* the faces of the men he had to fight. He thought of the *wedjat* amulet beneath his tunic. He prayed it would protect him—or at least grant him an honorable death.

The enemy halted. A gasp went up from the rebels.

Slowly, from the Crows' front line, came a monster of bronze, riding in a chariot drawn by two enormous black horses.

"Pharax," muttered the man beside Hylas. The name swept through the rebel lines faster than fear.

The Crow chieftain was faceless and inhuman: like a god. His cold, hollow voice rang out as he raised the dagger of Koronos. "The House of Koronos *cannot* be beaten! The gods Themselves have decreed that the enemy *shall be destroyed!*"

Hylas' spirit quailed, and around him, the rebels shrank back in terror. What if Pharax was right? What if *nothing* could beat the Crows, and the very gods were against them?

"No man is invincible!" called a clear, calm voice from farther up the line—and Akastos rode forward on Jinx. His armor shone, and the white crest on his helmet fluttered in the wind. He raised his sword and glanced around at his men. Unlike Pharax, his face could plainly be seen beneath his helmet, and it was resolute and unafraid. The power of his voice was so great that Hylas felt new courage coursing through him, and around him, men and boys gripped their weapons and took heart.

"No man is invincible!" repeated Akastos, leaping down from Jinx's back and hefting his oxhide shield as easily as if it were made of straw. "And no *man* can say for sure what it is that the gods have decreed—not even Pharax over there! *Especially* not Pharax! For what is he, beneath all that armor? Nothing but the son of the thief who stole Mycenae!"

Ripples of jittery laughter from the rebels.

"*I* am the rightful High Chieftain!" cried Akastos. "*I* am the Lion of Mycenae! When you fight for me, you fight for your farms and your fishing boats, your vineyards and your villages—you fight for your families and your loved ones! Follow me, I will lead you to victory!"

"The Lion of Mycenae has returned!" cried Periphas from the rear, and the rebels took up the cry: "The Lion of Mycenae has returned!"

And the battle began.

A blazing ball of pitch-soaked straw whizzed past Hylas and thudded onto a fallen shield. Thunder growled: The Sky Father was grinding the clouds to make a storm.

If only it would rain, thought Hylas. Then surely everyone will come to their senses and this will end?

The chaos was so great that he had no idea who was winning. He was staggering through a stink of blood and burst bowels: men screaming, arrows hissing, spears thudding into earth and hide and flesh. His mouth was dry, and beneath his unwieldy bronze armor he was pouring sweat—but there was no time for fear; it was all he could do to keep up with the rebels, while clumsily parrying blows with his heavy shield, and jabbing with his unfamiliar sword at whatever Crow warrior crossed his path.

A few paces ahead, Akastos was scything through the

Crows like a storm through barley. Hylas ran to catch up. A Crow warrior loomed in front of him and lunged at his chest with a spear. Hylas dodged sideways and hacked at the shaft, but his sword bounced off. Again the warrior lunged. Hylas darted behind the man and drove his blade through the gap between breastplate and straps, into his flank. The man gave a choking grunt and collapsed. Hylas felt the drag and suck as he yanked out his sword. The man lay where he'd fallen. He didn't move.

He's dead, thought Hylas numbly. I've killed him. He's dead. Blinking the sweat from his eyes, he stumbled after Akastos.

The High Chieftain was working his way toward Pharax, who'd leaped down from his chariot, and was stalking toward him on foot.

In the confusion, Akastos didn't see another Crow warrior leap at him from behind—but Hylas did. Racing forward, he dropped the warrior with a jab to the calf; Periphas leaped out from nowhere and finished the man off with his spear. Akastos acknowledged their help with a curt nod, and forged ahead.

Again Hylas struggled to catch up. Something struck him on the back of the head. The next moment, he was lying on the ground with his face in the dust. Spots floated before his eyes, blood trickled down his neck. He felt no pain, but when he tried to rise, his head whirled sickeningly; he couldn't get his balance.

At that moment, the sky went black. Hylas forgot his dizziness, he forgot everything. Dread darkened his mind. He heard a horse squealing in terror. He was dimly aware of men screaming, scattering in panic: *"The Angry Ones! The Angry Ones have come!"*

25

Telamon had been gone awhile, and still Hekabi hadn't burst in to set Pirra free. She'd heard the clatter of hooves in the courtyard as Telamon galloped away, and after that, silence.

"Hekabi?" she shouted. "*Hekabi,* I'm in here!"

Where *was* she? *Surely* she'd only been biding her time until Telamon was gone? Or had he brought men with him, who'd caught her—or killed her?

From behind Pirra came a sudden agitated scratching of falcon claws. Echo might be bound, hooded, and silenced, but she was frantically twisting her head this way and that. What new danger had she sensed?

A heartbeat later, Pirra smelled it too: fire. At the far end of the hall, smoke was curling around the doorway. With a sensation of falling, Pirra grasped why Hekabi hadn't come. The wisewoman had set fire to the eastern storerooms and then, thinking Pirra had done the same on the western side, she'd fled the stronghold, as they'd agreed. She must be up on the spur, waiting for Pirra, quite unaware that she was still inside, bound hand and foot.

"Hekabi!" Pirra shouted at the top of her voice. But she was deep in the heart of the stronghold. No matter how loud she screamed, nothing could reach Hekabi through so many cubits of stone.

Wildly, Pirra cast about her. Telamon had taken her knife; she could see no other weapon. Then she remembered the spear on the floor at the other end of the hall.

"I *will* come back for you!" she told Echo fiercely as she lay down and started wriggling across the floor.

It was painfully slow, kicking with her feet and boosting herself forward on her side, and by the time she was halfway down, she had to stop. Her breath stirred the ashes on the hearth. What a grim joke, she thought, that a fire that's been burning for generations should have died just as the entire stronghold's going up in flames.

She struggled on, trying to shut her mind to Echo's panicky scrabbling. A pall of gray smoke was thickening above her and she could hear a muffled roar, as if a monster were attacking the stronghold. She pictured the storerooms engulfed in flames: all those man-high jars of oil. *We'll need great heat for the fire to take hold,* Hekabi had said. And who would know more about setting a fire than she who worshipped the Lady of Fire?

At last, Pirra reached the spear. It was sharp bronze, but meant for jabbing, not sawing, and with her wrists tied behind her, she couldn't see what she was doing. The smoke was stinging her eyes and making her cough. At this rate, she'd never free herself in time.

Suddenly, she caught the patter of bare feet out in the passage. "In here!" she croaked.

A figure appeared in the smoke.

Astonished, Pirra took in the sullen features of one of her Marsh Dweller guides: The mute boy she'd nicknamed Stone. "Quick, cut me free!" she gasped.

The boy stood scowling in the doorway. He still wore his fish skin head-binding, but he'd washed the mud off his face and his features looked more delicate and childlike.

"*Hurry!*" shouted Pirra. "Echo's tied up at the other end of the hall, we've got to get out of here!"

Still the boy hesitated. Something about him was oddly familiar: those eyes, and that tuft of barley-colored hair poking out from his head-binding . . .

It can't be, thought Pirra. Then she saw the knife at his hip—and the frog carved on the hilt.

"*Issi?*" she said.

Issi stared at Pirra with Hylas' clear tawny eyes. Now that Pirra had realized, the resemblance was startling. Here was Hylas' younger self—except that this girl was mute and suspicious, a child of eleven summers, scarred by too long alone and on the run.

"Issi, *please,* cut me free!"

Still scowling, Issi drew her knife and set to work on Pirra's wrists.

"Why didn't you *tell* me?" said Pirra, rubbing the feeling back into her hands.

Issi ignored her and started on her ankles. The last rope snapped. Pirra tried to stand, but her legs gave way. She grabbed the doorway for support. "Fetch Echo," she gasped, "but *don't* untie her till we're outside, or she'll panic and never find her way out—"

Issi shot her a glance that was incredibly like Hylas: *Of course I won't, I'm not an idiot!*—then headed off at a crouching run under the smoke, returning soon after with Echo cradled in her arms.

Blindly, they staggered out into the passageway, into a nightmare of scorching black smoke. As Pirra held her breath, she tried not to think about Echo and whether she was still alive.

At last they burst into the courtyard: more roiling smoke, and a deafening roar. Bent double with her hands on her knees, Pirra took great heaving gulps of air. She saw Issi cut Echo's bonds, then slip off the falcon's hood and throw her to the wind.

Echo recovered in an instant and shot skyward. As Pirra watched her hurtle out of danger, some of the tightness in her chest snapped loose, and she breathed more easily.

Huge orange flames were pouring out of the storerooms and attacking the roof—but now, beneath the roar, Pirra caught the frantic screams of donkeys and horses.

She and Issi exchanged horrified stares. In Hekabi's single-minded urge for vengeance, she'd forgotten to open the stable doors and set the animals free.

Pirra and Issi slid off the horse's back and collapsed, coughing and retching in the grass.

Below them the roof of a watchtower caved in with a crash, sending great jets of flame roaring skyward. The horse squealed in terror. Hekabi grabbed the reins and tied it to a thorn tree.

"That's the last of them," panted Pirra on hands and knees.

"Here," said Hekabi, tossing her the waterskin. Like them, she was covered in soot; when Pirra hadn't met her on the spur, she'd returned to Lapithos, and found them desperately freeing the frantic animals.

Pirra gulped a mouthful, then passed the waterskin to Issi, who was crouching in the grass, blinking owlishly. In the child's small pointed face, Pirra saw the same mute distrust as before. Except it's more than that, thought Pirra in puzzlement, it's almost—hostility.

She turned to Hekabi. "Have you known about her all along?"

"Of course not," said the wisewoman, never taking her eyes off the blazing stronghold. "I told you, I thought the shadow thief was a boy . . ."

Great charcoal thunderclouds were darkening the sky, lit from within by flickers of lightning—and yet no rain fell. The gods Themselves were letting Lapithos burn.

"But did you really never suspect—"

"While I was waiting for you," Hekabi cut in, still

watching the fire, "I saw a Crow warrior on a horse: a boy, heading down the mountain. Was that Telamon?"

Another paroxysm of coughing seized Pirra: She could only nod. When she could speak again, she told the wisewoman what had happened in the stronghold. "Koronos is dead," she croaked.

"*Dead*," gloated Hekabi. "My curse is beginning to work."

"Maybe—but Telamon has a plan. I'm not sure what he means to do, but he said that if it succeeds, no one will be able to reach the dagger—it'll be safe forever! He said . . ." Again she broke off to cough.

Impatiently, Hekabi waited for her to go on. Even Issi crept closer to listen.

In bursts, Pirra told Hekabi everything Telamon had said. "He's going to give it to his Ancestors. But what does that *mean*?"

Firelight danced in the wisewoman's dark eyes. "The Ancestor Peak," she muttered. "Issi, you know Mount Lykas: Is it true that above the tomb there's a crack in the peak? A crack that reaches right down into the heart of the mountain?"

Issi nodded.

"That's it!" cried Hekabi. "If he threw the dagger down there—"

"We'd never get it out!" exclaimed Pirra. "It would be safe with his Ancestors forever!"

They stared at each other.

"But he might not get his hands on it," said Pirra. "First he'll have to find Pharax in the middle of the battle, then he'll have to take it off him: How likely is that?"

"True," said Hekabi. "But I have a feeling that he will. This has a whiff of destiny about it."

Pirra's thoughts raced as she watched Echo soaring overhead. If Hekabi was right and Telamon did get the dagger, they had to go up the mountain and stop him flinging it down the crack. But they didn't know the way.

Suddenly, she snapped her fingers. "Issi knows how to get there! Issi, you have to take us . . . Issi? *Issi!*"

The hillside was empty. Issi was gone.

26

The din of battle had fallen away, and all Hylas could hear was his harsh panting breath as he stared at the Angry Ones wheeling overhead. He saw Them more clearly than he ever had before: Their vast wings and writhing necks, Their raw red mouths like gaping wounds.

He was still on the ground where he'd fallen after the blow to the head, and his legs still wouldn't work. Not far in front of him, he made out Pharax and Akastos. Akastos glanced up at the Angry Ones and faltered, dread convulsing his hard features. But Hekabi's charm still hung on its thong around his neck, and he gathered his courage and stalked on to meet his enemy. Pharax seemed scarcely to regard the spirits of vengeance: He feared nothing while he held the dagger of Koronos.

He was a head taller than Akastos, and faceless in his high neck-guard and his helmet with its jagged horn crest. Akastos was less heavily clad and swifter, circling and forcing his enemy to twist and turn.

Akastos thrust his left forearm through his shield

handle so that he could fight two-handed, and began changing his sword from left to right, to disconcert his opponent. Pharax too thrust his left forearm through his shield, but he had both the dagger of Koronos and a massive thrusting spear three armspans long that vastly extended his reach.

He lunged with the spear. Akastos dodged, Pharax stabbed with the dagger; but the blade glanced harmlessly off the lion on Akastos' breastplate. More blows and counter-blows too fast to follow.

Suddenly, Akastos sank to the ground. Hylas stared in horror. Akastos was clutching his side. Pharax's spear had found its mark.

"Akastos!" yelled Hylas, struggling to his knees.

Pharax loomed over the High Chieftain with the dagger raised for the kill.

"Akastos," whispered Hylas.

But as Pharax made to deal the death blow, Akastos, baring his teeth in a grimace of pain, hefted his sword, drove it sharply upward—and skewered the Crow Chieftain through the groin. With a dreadful howl, Pharax pitched backward, and the dagger of Koronos flew from his fist. Hylas saw it land not far from where he knelt. He struggled to his feet and lurched forward. But Pharax wasn't finished yet: He too was crawling toward the dagger.

From the corner of his eye, Hylas saw Akastos grab Pharax's fallen spear. With the last of his strength, the High Chieftain cast the spear. It hissed past Hylas, and with lethal accuracy it found the hair-thin gap between Pharax's breastplate and shoulder-guard, and pinned him to the ground.

Akastos slumped back, breathing through clenched teeth. Pharax writhed in his death throes in a spreading pool of blood. Hylas saw the Crow leader claw the earth a whisker from the dagger—then his hand went still. Pharax was dead.

Hylas stared at the blood around the corpse. *The lifeblood of a highborn Crow . . .*

Above him, the Angry Ones were circling: But why didn't They swoop down and *drink*? For fifteen long years, Akastos had labored to appease his brother's ghost and rid himself of the Angry Ones with the blood of a highborn Crow—so why wasn't it working?

Then Hylas saw Hekabi's charm on the High Chieftain's chest. Was that keeping the Angry Ones at bay?

The dagger of Koronos could wait. Staggering over to Akastos, Hylas fell to his knees and ripped the charm from the High Chieftain's breast, then he flung it as far as he could.

"Spirits of air and darkness!" he yelled. *"There is the lifeblood of Pharax, son of Koronos! Drink—and leave Akastos in peace forever!"*

Like monstrous vultures, the Angry Ones dropped out of the sky and thudded to earth. Hylas heard the leathery rustle of wings and smelled the stink of charred flesh. He saw Their serpentine necks bent over the scarlet pool in which Pharax lay. He heard the dreadful, greedy sounds as They sucked the blood of vengeance.

Then he became aware of a gray human shape among the vast, jostling wings: a warrior on his knees, also stooping over the blood, and greedily lapping. Hylas clutched the *wedjat* amulet on his chest, but he couldn't look away.

The ghost of Akastos' murdered brother resembled the High Chieftain, only it was younger, and missing the little finger on its right hand. Slowly, it straightened, licking the blood from its lips and staring ahead with the vacant gaze of one still thirsty. Then it bent its head for more.

With a *thwap*, the Angry Ones lifted into the sky and veered off toward Mount Lykas.

Akastos moaned. His face was ghastly pale, and his eyes were shut.

"It's finished," said Hylas through a blur of tears. "You've atoned for your crime, the Angry Ones have gone. Be at peace!"

Akastos' face twisted in pain, and he didn't open his eyes. His long punishment was over, but it didn't look as if he would live to enjoy it.

As Hylas knelt, blinking down at the man he'd loved as a father, the din of battle crashed upon him once more, and he became aware of what was happening around him. He saw the dagger of Koronos lying almost within his reach. He heard Periphas somewhere behind him, yelling his name in warning. Then a Crow warrior was looming out of the smoke, with his spear raised to deal Akastos his death blow.

Grabbing the High Chieftain's shield, Hylas parried the blow. The Crow warrior screamed as Periphas' sword pierced his back—and fell dead, crushing Hylas beneath him.

For a moment, Hylas lay winded. As he struggled to free himself and reach the dagger of Koronos, he heard a horse galloping toward him.

A horse? he thought dazedly. But Jinx cantered off the battlefield after Akastos dismounted, I saw him go . . .

Hylas couldn't see who it was because of the corpse on top of him, but he heard the horse skitter to a halt, somewhere close. Then its rider leaped off and strode into view. It was Telamon.

Before Hylas could take in what was happening, Telamon had spotted the dagger and was striding toward it. He only had eyes for his prize, he didn't see Hylas beneath the warrior's corpse. Snatching the dagger from the ground, he cast a scornful glance at the motionless forms of Pharax and Akastos. Then he leaped back on his horse and raised the dagger high.

"*Akastos is dead!*" he roared. "*Pharax is no more, and I, Telamon, am High Chieftain of all Akea! See! I have the dagger of Koronos!*"

Shouts went up from his men, and the rebels cried out in dismay.

Telamon's horse reared, but he checked it, and shouted

orders to his second-in-command: "Ilarkos! You will lead our men to victory here—while I ride to make the dagger safe for my House for all eternity!"

Before Hylas could free himself, Telamon was galloping across the battlefield, yelling in triumph and brandishing the dagger of Koronos above his head.

27

Pirra reined in her horse in a cloud of dust. From below her came a raucous din: She was nearing the battlefield.

Her body was screaming for rest, and her mount was heaving and blowing after its headlong gallop from Lapithos. Maybe somewhere the Sun was still shining, but thunderclouds shrouded Lykonia in menacing gloom, and it was so hot, she could hardly breathe. Surely the storm would break soon?

In the distance, a voice was shouting: *"I will make the dagger safe for all eternity!"* It was Telamon. He sounded triumphant.

Wildly, Pirra cast about, but she couldn't tell where he was, and when he shouted again, he sounded much farther away. Setting her teeth, she urged her horse toward the battlefield.

The din grew louder. Through a haze of dirty brown smoke, she saw smashed shields and scattered fires, men sprawled or twitching horribly, waves of warriors and rebels crashing against each other. *Where was Hylas?*

She spotted him in a group of rebels making for the edge of the field not fifty paces to her right. He'd lost his helmet and his face was bloodied, but he was grimly alive, limping beside a black-maned horse on whose back lay Akastos—whether dead or unconscious, Pirra couldn't tell.

As she put her horse toward them, she saw Periphas run from the smoke, push back Akastos' hair, and peer at his face.

"He's still breathing!" he yelled. "Nomios, get him to safety! The rest of you, come with me! The battle is *not* lost, we have everything to fight for!"

Hylas turned on him. "But Telamon has the dagger! I couldn't stop him!"

"And I know where he's taking it!" cried Pirra, cantering down to them.

They stared at her, and it flashed across her mind how she must appear: a wild-haired girl covered in soot on an exhausted horse lathered in sweat.

"He's taking it to his Ancestors!" she panted. "Hekabi thinks he's going to throw it down the crack in the Ancestor Peak—then it'll be safe forever!" She was about to add that Issi was up there too, maybe heading for the Ancestor Peak, to try and stop him—but Hylas had enough to deal with, without learning that Pirra had found his sister, only to lose her again.

"Hekabi's right," Hylas said in an altered voice. "That has to be what Telamon meant. He's going to throw it to his Ancestors."

"This peak, do you know the way?" said Pirra.

He didn't reply. He was appraising her exhausted horse, and she guessed what he was thinking: It would never make it up the mountain.

"Take Jinx," said Periphas. "We'll use the girl's horse for Akastos."

The swap was swiftly made, Periphas gently easing the wounded man off the black-maned horse called Jinx.

Hylas jerked his head at Pirra. "You get up first."

"What? But he'll be slower with two of us—"

"I'm not leaving you on a battlefield!" Boosting her onto the horse's back, he jumped up behind her and gathered the reins.

As if to mark his words, a great shout rang out behind them, and the Crow warriors attacked with fresh savagery. Pirra recognized their leader as Ilarkos, a ruthless warrior who she knew would fight to the death. The rebels knew it too. Pharax might be dead, but Telamon had the dagger, and Pirra saw the weariness in their grimy faces; even Periphas' shoulders sagged.

"Do you see that red glare in the foothills?" she shouted while Jinx snorted and sidestepped. "That's Lapithos! We set it on fire! And listen to this, all of you! Koronos is dead!"

"*Dead?*" cried Periphas in disbelief.

Pirra nodded. "It's true, I saw his corpse!"

With shining eyes, Periphas raised his sword. "Koronos is *dead*!" he roared, and the rebels within earshot took up the cry. "*Koronos is dead!*"

"Hold tight," Hylas muttered in Pirra's ear. As she grabbed fistfuls of Jinx's coarse black mane, Hylas yanked the horse's head around and dug in his heels.

—❦—

"How much farther d'you think Jinx can take us?" panted Pirra.

"Top of that ridge," said Hylas. "From there it's too steep, I'll have to continue on foot."

Pirra noticed that he said "I," not "we," but she made no remark. She asked how he knew that Telamon was going the same way, and he said, "Because this is the shortest trail, and I've seen his tracks."

They'd slowed to a jolting trot as Jinx picked his way up a stony trail between tall pines. With a double load, the stallion was tiring fast: Several times, he'd stumbled and nearly pitched them over his head.

For the tenth time, Pirra debated whether to tell Hylas that she'd found Issi. He ought to be told—and yet what *good* would it do? It might prove a fatal distraction, at a time when he needed all his wits to stay alive . . .

They came to a stream, and of one accord slid off and fell to their knees to drink, while Jinx threw down his head and took long thirsty slurps.

A crash of thunder, and the stallion jerked up his head. "Why won't the storm *break*?" muttered Hylas. He glanced at Pirra. "Did you really set fire to Lapithos?"

She wiped her mouth on the back of her hand. "Hekabi did, I just helped. She's still up there; she said the main thing was for me to take the horse and find you."

"*The House of Koronos burns . . .*" muttered Hylas. "But I haven't wielded the dagger."

"Not yet," said Pirra.

As he rose to his feet, he asked if she'd seen Havoc, and she nodded. "Echo was with her; I think she's looking forward to the storm." She flashed him a grin, but he didn't smile back. His face was gaunt with fatigue and there was a darkness in his eyes that she'd never seen before. She wondered what horrors he'd experienced on the battlefield.

Suddenly, she knew that she had to tell him about Issi. He needed to know that his sister was alive, in case—in case Hekabi's prediction came true, and he was killed.

"Hylas," she began, "there's something I—"

"Jinx can't carry the two of us any farther," he blurted out.

"What?"

"You know that, don't you?" His face was drawn and determined as he picked up the reins. "You have to stay here, Pirra, where it's safe. I have to go after Telamon alone."

Despite the heat, she'd gone cold. "Then—you'd better go, hadn't you?" she said shakily.

For a heartbeat he met her eyes. He gave a curt nod and prepared to mount—but then he turned and pulled her into his arms. It hurt because of his breastplate, but she didn't care. She breathed his smell of forest and horse and sweat; she raised her head and kissed his mouth, and he kissed her back, hard. Then he leaped up on Jinx and cantered off.

Pirra fixed her eyes stubbornly on the ground: She *would not* watch him go. Then she changed her mind—but she was too late; already he was out of sight among the pines.

Pirra sniffed and wiped her eyes with her fingers. She knelt and retied her sandal. Then she started up the trail, after him.

It was only then that she realized that somehow, before he left, Hylas had managed to take off his *wedjat* amulet and slip it over her head: So now she had a powerful charm to keep her safe—while he had none.

Telamon's horse was stumbling with exhaustion, but still he kept beating its flanks with his stick. He'd nearly reached the end of the trail: Nothing could stop him now. Koronos was dead. So was Pharax, and Akastos— the so-called Lion of Mycenae. The gods had chosen him, Telamon, to rule.

Above him, the Ancestor Peak loomed blood-red against the charcoal clouds. Below him in the foothills, he glimpsed a blaze of orange flame. Earlier, his horse had shied in terror as he'd galloped past the fiery chaos that Lapithos had become, and for a moment, his courage had faltered. *"The House of Koronos burns,"* the Oracle had said . . .

But *I* have the dagger, not Hylas, he'd told himself. So

what if Lapithos is burning? I'll have it rebuilt, bigger and more splendid than before.

He'd felt a fleeting regret for Pirra, shut up inside—but so be it. It was her fate to die; it wasn't his fault.

A crash of thunder and a blinding flare of lightning showed him the end of the trail. His horse reared, nearly pitching him off, and he yanked savagely at the reins.

That was when he saw it: someone—some*thing*—crouching above him on the trail. In the gloom, he made out a small hunched form and a sharp gray face. Tawny eyes glaring at him through a thatch of barley-colored hair.

"*Issi?*" he croaked. But it *couldn't* be her. Issi was dead, she had to be.

Then from high overhead came a rushing sound, as of vast leathery wings. His horse squealed in terror; he struggled to control it. When he looked again, Issi's ghost was gone.

Springing down, he ran to the place where she'd been—but he could find no tracks. He went cold. *Ghosts,* he thought.

Whipping out the dagger, he slashed at the empty air. Was his father's ghost here too? And Alekto's? And Pharax's and Koronos'?

"I never touched any of you!" he whispered. "The gods *wanted* you to die!"

More thunder, more lightning. Wildly, he glared at the churning black clouds. Were the Angry Ones wheeling above him? *Were They following him up the mountain?*

The sight of the iron ring on his finger gave him courage. Not even the Angry Ones could touch him. Nothing could. Now only Hylas was left, and he was far below on the plain, perhaps already slaughtered in battle.

As lightning flared around him, Telamon felt a tingling in his bronze breastplate, and the power of the dagger coursed through him. His will hardened. It would be a wrench to fling the dagger down the chasm of his Ancestors, but he would do it.

He was Telamon, High Chieftain of Mycenae. He could do anything.

28

The she-lion leaped onto a boulder and anxiously snuffed the wind, while below her the little human cub picked her way between the pines, completely unaware of the dangers around her.

The fires in the Up were making the she-lion's claws tingle and her fur stand on end. Soon all that rage in the Up would send the wet hammering down. But while most creatures had taken shelter in caves or the forest, the little human was determinedly following the evil crow-man on the horse. *Why?* What was on top of the mountain?

Twitching her tail in frustration, the she-lion bounded after her charge. If only the little human would stay *out* of danger, instead of going to look for it! The she-lion had led her right to the girl and the female with the magpie mane, who could have kept her safe—but instead, the little human had watched from her hiding place, then sneaked *right into the crow-men's burning lair.*

And just now, she'd nearly gotten trampled by that horse. The she-lion had had to knock her over and push her into some bushes, but even this hadn't put her off. She

didn't seem to care about the crow-man's big shiny claw—
and she seemed not to have sensed the far greater menace
that was following *him*.

The she-lion had often sensed the terror that haunted
the Up, and she'd caught Their black, biting stink. She
feared no living creature—but she feared the terrible
winged spirits of the Up.

Strangely, humans couldn't see them very well, although
like horses, they often panicked when they were near. Just
now, the she-lion had watched the crow-man slashing
frantically at the Up. How odd that he hadn't seen the
terrible spirit perched on a boulder, only a paw-swipe
behind him.

As for the little human cub, she was frightened of them
too, but not nearly frightened enough. She didn't seem to
realize that the terrible spirits don't *care* who is good and
who is bad—or who gets in Their way.

The little human had climbed out of sight around a
bend, and the she-lion hurried after her. The nose-biting
stink thickened—the entire mountainside reeked—and up
ahead, she caught the rustle of giant wings and the scratch
of talons on stone.

Rounding the bend, she saw to her horror a whole
shadowy swarm of them, hunched on boulders a few
pounces up the slope. *And the little human was climbing
blindly toward Them.*

The she-lion shot up the slope and leaped in front
of her, roaring at the spirits and lashing out with both

forepaws. They spread Their vast wings and screeched at her, blasting her back with Their burning breath—but They didn't fly away. One lone she-lion wasn't enough to drive Them off.

Still roaring, the she-lion spun around and swatted the little human downhill into a patch of thistles. With an outraged yelp, the little human struggled to her feet. She was furious and frightened, but still grimly determined to head *back* into danger.

The she-lion bounded down and leaned firmly against her. *No, not that way!* The little human tried to push her aside, which was ridiculous; it was like being pushed by a leaf.

Gently, the she-lion took one small furless forepaw in her jaws and tugged—and at last, the cub understood, and started up a different trail that looped *around* the boulders where the terrible spirits perched. As the she-lion followed her, snaky necks twisted to watch them go, and she heard the rustle as the terrible spirits folded Their wings. The danger was past—for now.

The she-lion had to keep her charge safe, until she could find the rest of the pride; but she needed help. She couldn't fight these spirits on her own. And she couldn't fly.

―――

The falcon had had a *marvelous* kill. After one of her fastest dives *ever,* she'd knocked a big fat pigeon out of the Sky and caught it in her talons just before it hit the ground, then she'd swooped onto a rock, ripped out its breast feathers, and gulped its salty-sweet flesh. After that she'd felt sluggish and full, but she'd soon sicked up a large pellet, and squirted a massive load of droppings—and now she felt light and fast again, and ready for anything.

No more screeching at ants, no more being shivery and scared and unfalcon-like. Best of all, no more awfulness of being *tied up* and unable to see, or move so much as a feather. All that was behind her. She was a falcon again, with the limitless Sky for her home.

And she was thoroughly enjoying this storm. The lightning tickled her nostrils and set up a delicious tingling at the roots of her feathers; the Wind was fascinatingly bumpy, and there were all sorts of rock-hard clouds and wobbly towers of air for her to zoom around and in between.

Far below her on the plains, she scanned the poor earthbound humans, slogging away at their fighting. They were so slow and so *angry*. Near the top of the mountain, she spotted the evil crow-human who'd had the effrontery to trap her in his stinking black wings, then tie her up. With a shudder of disgust, she swooped past him—and of course he didn't see her, because like all humans, he kept his head down as he plodded toward the peak.

Scornfully, the falcon slid sideways on the Wind—and nearly crashed into a swarm of the dreadful, bat-winged spirits.

Badly shaken, she shot off across the Sky. The spirits ignored her, screeching and twisting Their long black necks to peer at the tiny, toiling crow-human below.

The falcon was scared. She longed to fly away and never

come back. There were lots of other mountains just as good as this one, that weren't haunted by the terrible spirits; and she could go wherever she liked in the flick of a feather.

But. The girl was on *this* mountain—and she too was nearing the top. So was the boy. And there was his little sister, the one who'd freed the falcon from the fire; and with her was the she-lion, who could usually look after herself—but not this time. This time, even the she-lion needed help.

As the falcon spiraled higher on an updraft, she felt the girl's fear of the crow-humans, and her gnawing anxiety for the boy. The falcon *hated* it when the girl was worried, because then she was worried too.

A thunderclap and a flare of lightning—and at last the clouds burst and the rain pelted down.

Reluctantly, the falcon tilted one wing feather and swerved, and headed back toward the mountain.

Sleeking back her feathers, she flew into the spirits' dreadful reek. Their screams drove spikes through her skull and terror into her heart. She saw the rain hissing and turning to smoke on Their vast, scorching, featherless wings . . .

The falcon knew that she could fly faster than any living creature—faster even than Them—but They were many, and so huge.

Against such terrible beings, what could even a falcon do?

29

When Hylas was eleven, his best friend Telamon announced that he was going to climb the Ancestor Peak, and would Hylas come and watch him do it?

The Ancestor Peak was forbidden, they'd never even been there—but that was the point. So Hylas had left Issi with the goats, and he and Telamon had taken the little-used trail up the mountain to its uppermost shoulder, where they'd stood craning their necks at the raw red peak. Around them, tall black pines creaked in the wind, guarding a narrow walled-in doorway cut into the rock.

"That must be the Tomb of the Ancestors," said Telamon in a low voice.

"Whose Ancestors?" muttered Hylas.

"Not sure, but I think they're mine. Father never talks about our kin. All I know is they're in the north. Mycenae, I think it's called."

"Mm," mumbled Hylas, studying the peak. "You really want to do this?" Telamon was a summer older than him, and bigger because he got more food—but still. To climb this peak, you'd have to scramble up the naked rock above that tomb, then all the way up those footholds that someone had hacked out; and *then,* near the top, you'd have to cross that crack, where some god had split the peak with his ax. And you'd have to manage all that while the wind was doing its best to blow you off.

Telamon was fiddling with his sealstone. He cleared his throat. "I'll climb it if you come too," he mumbled.

Hylas shot him a look. Then he broke into a grin. "All right. Let's do it!"

And they had. It had been a bright morning in spring. A swallow had whizzed past Hylas' head as he'd climbed the sun-hot rock, his heart thudding against his ribs, his senses fizzing and alert . . . And when they'd done it and scrambled back to the pines, they'd collapsed against each other, spluttering with jittery laughter and promising eternal friendship.

Lightning flashed and Hylas' breastplate tingled; then a crash of thunder burst the clouds and at last the rain hammered down: In moments he was soaked and the trail was running with mud. His breastplate was still tingling. Something flickered in his memory, something Akastos had said once . . . but before he could grasp it, it was gone.

Around him, storm-tossed trees thrashed and roared, and somewhere below, Jinx whinnied. An answering whinny from above, then Telamon's riderless horse came careening down the trail, nearly knocking Hylas over in its haste to escape.

So Telamon was already up there. Hylas pictured him

casting the dagger down the crack, for the Ancestors to keep forever.

At last, he reached the grove of black pines. No Telamon. Slitting his eyes against the rain, Hylas made out the door to the Tomb of the House of Koronos. A lightning-struck pine had toppled against one side of it, making a spiky ladder that led up to its rocky roof.

Another flare of lightning—and there was Telamon, standing at the foot of the fallen pine. He hadn't seen Hylas: He was holding the dagger of Koronos before him, gazing at it with longing and regret. Hylas guessed that he was summoning the will to climb the peak and fling away his prize.

Telamon felt Hylas' stare and turned, and drew his sword.

Hylas had already drawn his sword and his Egyptian knife, so they had two weapons apiece. "An even match," he called as he advanced on his erstwhile friend.

"Hardly," sneered Telamon. "I'm a warrior, you're just an Outsi—"

"But I've fought a battle and you haven't."

Telamon lunged at him. Hylas dodged, but not far enough; Telamon aimed a kick at his sword hand and knocked his weapon out of his grip. The sword clattered down the trail, and Telamon grinned. "Not so even now, is it?"

They circled each other, silver jets of rain bouncing off their armor. Hylas feinted at Telamon, who fell to one knee, dropping his sword. Hylas flicked it away with his knife. He'd meant to grab it, but he flicked it too far, and it also clattered out of reach.

Meanwhile, Telamon had lost no time in starting up the pine trunk that led to the roof of the tomb.

"I wouldn't do it, Telamon!" shouted Hylas, heading after him. "Now you've only got the dagger: If you chuck it down that crack, you'll have no weapons left! You won't live very long with me on your tail!"

"But if I throw it to my Ancestors," panted Telamon over his shoulder, "I'll be invincible!"

Hylas barked a laugh. "You want to put that to the test, do you? You with no weapons and me with a knife?"

Telamon ignored him, lurching up the slippery trunk that was spiked with broken branches.

Hylas was halfway up it when he caught movement above Telamon. Through the driving rain, he saw Havoc, drenched, clinging precariously to the streaming rocks. And just below her, waiting to ambush Telamon, crouched a huddled figure clutching a knife.

Time stopped. Hylas forgot the wind and the rain, he even forgot Telamon as he stared up at a shock of barley-colored hair and a small fierce face he hadn't seen in two summers.

She stared down at him, openmouthed.

His lips formed her name, but no sound came. *Issi* . . .

"Hylas, look out!" screamed Pirra from somewhere below.

He threw himself sideways, and Telamon's knife-thrust

missed his neck, glanced off his breastplate, and struck his forearm instead. He dropped his Egyptian knife; Telamon snatched it with a triumphant shout. "Now I have *two* weapons and you have none!" Wobbling on the tree trunk, he lunged for the kill, but Hylas had backed down, out of range.

"Coward!" taunted Telamon, climbing higher. He saw Issi and faltered. She ducked behind a rock. Havoc sprang at him. But the lioness had misjudged the distance and she fell short, her claws scrabbling for a grip on the slippery stone. As Hylas watched in horror, the lioness slid with a dreadful scraping sound and disappeared down the other side of the peak.

Hylas stopped breathing. Havoc didn't reappear. He couldn't remember what was on that side of the peak: Were there trees, to break her fall? Or was there nothing but a sheer drop off the mountain?

Above him, Telamon was hooting with glee. "The gods are on *my* side, Hylas! Not even your lion can help you now!" He sprang off the pine trunk onto the first of the footholds hacked in the rock, heaved the tree over, and sent it crashing toward Hylas.

Hylas leaped clear in time—but down at the tomb, Pirra screamed. She seemed to have jumped aside, but not quickly enough, a branch had fallen across her leg and pinned her to the ground. Hylas saw her struggling to free herself. But he couldn't go and help her; he had to stop Telamon from reaching the crack.

As Hylas started up the footholds, the sky suddenly darkened, and the Ancestor Peak was blotted out by vast, charred wings. The reeking breath of the Angry Ones scorched Hylas' lungs. Their screams pierced his brain and froze his heart with dread. They were everywhere: menacing Telamon above, and Issi cowering behind her rock; even swooping lower to attack Pirra, down at the tomb.

Telamon was lashing out blindly at the terror in the sky, clutching Hylas' knife in one hand and the dagger of Koronos in the other. He'd nearly reached the crack that split the Ancestor Peak and led to the fathomless heart of Mount Lykas.

Then Hylas heard a sound like tearing silk, and a dark bolt plummeted past him. Below him, the Angry Ones drew apart with stone-splitting screeches, and Echo swooped around and harried Them again, shrieking and twisting nimbly out of reach as she chased Them away from Issi behind her rock, then hurtled lower to attack those threatening Pirra at the tomb.

More Angry Ones were circling the peak like gigantic vultures. "They're coming for you, Telamon!" panted Hylas, toiling after him. "You can't see them, but I can! The Angry Ones are all around you!"

"You're lying!" yelled Telamon. But his face was wild with terror and his long hair flew as he cast about him.

"They're after you! You left Alekto to the crocodiles!"

"I never *touched* her!" screamed Telamon. "The Angry Ones *can't* hurt me, not while I have my ring of iron!"

Another flare of lightning set Hylas' breastplate tingling—and at last he remembered what Akastos had told him, back in the smithy on Thalakrea: *Bronze draws the power of the gods . . .*

Telamon was within a few steps of the crack. Somehow, Hylas had to keep him there while the thunder and lightning stalked ever nearer . . .

"Telamon!" he cried, ripping at the thongs that fastened his breastplate to his chest. "You swore to the Angry Ones that you'd cut out my heart! Well, here it is!" Wrenching off his armor, he flung it down the mountain; then he ripped open his tunic and bared his chest. "Look, Telamon, I'm unarmed and unprotected! Now's your chance!"

In disbelief, Telamon watched Hylas starting toward him. "Don't come any closer, Hylas, I know it's a trick!" But as he turned to climb the final steps to the crack, he slipped and lost his grip on the dagger.

Another flare of lightning, so close that Hylas caught the stink of burned stone—and there was Issi, snatching the dagger from the step.

"*No Issi, no!*" he bellowed. "Put it *down*, let Telamon have it! Get *down*, Issi, *down*!"

Issi met his eyes in astonishment—then she did as he said, dropping the dagger on the step and half sliding, half falling past him down the rocks.

With a shout of triumph, Telamon snatched the bronze dagger and raised it high. "The Outsider didn't wield it very long, did she?" he yelled.

"Long enough to fulfill the Oracle," panted Hylas, to keep him talking. "The House of Koronos—Lapithos— it's burning, Telamon, just like the Oracle said! You must have seen it on your way up!"

"*I* am the House of Koronos," roared Telamon, straddling the crack that led down to his Ancestors. "*I am invincible!*"

The pain in Hylas' temples grew unbearable, and he saw the Angry Ones blackening the sky above Telamon.

"*I am invincible!*" he roared again.

The Angry Ones shrieked and scattered. Hylas saw a blinding light and the clouds splitting open, a vast shining fist hurling a bolt of dazzling fire at the peak. At the same moment, Havoc leaped at his chest, knocking him out of the path of the lightning. He heard Telamon scream as the bolt struck the dagger of Koronos and blasted him off the peak.

Then the whole sky was ablaze and Hylas slid down into blackness—and saw nothing at all.

30

Hylas woke up lying on his back. He was battered and bruised all over and his face felt sunburned and stiff. He couldn't open his eyes: His eyelids were stuck together.

He was lying in wet bracken. He heard dripping and trickling. An owl hooted. Shards of memory returned. A blinding glare, Telamon brandishing the dagger as lightning blasted him from the peak.

"Pirra?" croaked Hylas. "Issi! Havoc! Anyone?"

No answer.

Blindly, he rolled onto all fours and began to crawl. He hadn't gone far when his hand touched cold, dead flesh. He smelled charred skin. His reluctant fingers moved over long braids with tiny discs at the ends. He found Telamon's lifeless fist clenching a stump of twisted metal: What remained of the dagger of Koronos.

If the Outsider wields the blade, the House of Koronos burns. The Oracle had been fulfilled—but the words of the gods never mean quite what you think. It was Issi who'd wielded the blade, and it was Telamon who'd burned. *I am the House of Koronos,* he'd screamed—and retribution had come from the sky. Hylas remembered Thestor's ghost pointing its finger upward, in warning. The gods had blasted Telamon and the dagger to oblivion. The rule of the Crows was over.

It was what Hylas had fought for, but he felt too numb to take it in.

Something stirred in the bracken, and he heard a large creature moving toward him. Then Havoc was making groany *owmp owmp* noises and thrusting her whiskery muzzle in his face.

A sob rose in his throat. He flung his arms around her neck and buried his head in her fur. If she hadn't knocked him out of the path of the lightning, he would be as dead as Telamon.

Someone else was here too, but he couldn't see them, his eyelids were still stuck together. "Who's there?" he gasped.

A small cool hand touched his.

"Pirra?"

An angry hiss, and whoever it was ran off.

"*Issi!*" shouted Hylas. "Issi come *back*!"

After that he must have lost consciousness, because when he woke again, he could feel the heat of the Sun, although he still couldn't open his eyes.

A bird lit onto a branch, spattering him with raindrops. He caught the faint breeze of Echo's wings as she flew down to him with an ear-splitting *Kyi! Kyi!*

He heard an answering cry—then Pirra was crashing

through the bracken. "Well done, Echo!" she panted. She was kneeling beside him, laughing and sniffing and giving him little pats on his shoulders and chest. "Thank the Goddess you're *alive*, we've been looking everywhere, we couldn't *find* you!"

"Where's Issi? Is she all right?"

"She's fine, I saw her just now with Havoc. But Hylas, your face—you look as if you've got sunburn!"

"The lightning was so close. I—I can't open my eyes. What about you?"

"My ankle's all swollen, I'm hopping with a stick."

"Did you see—Telamon's here too."

"I know," she said in an altered voice. "Can you sense his ghost?"

". . . No. No, I can't."

"It's over, Hylas. The gods destroyed the dagger. There's only what's left in his fist, the rest was shattered to bits."

Hylas did not reply. Koronos, Pharax, Telamon . . . All dead. But he couldn't feel glad. He was sick of death.

Pirra gave his shoulder another pat. "We've got to get you down the mountain."

She helped him to his feet, and at last his eyelids came unstuck and he blinked. He blinked again. He touched his eyelids. They were flaky and dry, but definitely open. He felt hollow inside, as if he were falling from a great height.

"Can you walk if you lean on me?" said Pirra.

"I can walk all right, but . . . Everything's black."

"What do you mean?"

"Pirra, everything's *black*. I can't see."

The battle had ended soon after Hylas and Pirra had left.

"Our luck changed," said Periphas, "when Pirra told us Koronos was dead. Then Hekabi saw lightning strike Mount Lykas; she shouted it was a sign the gods were against the Crows. Soon afterward, the battle turned, and Ilarkos and his men realized it was hopeless, and surrendered."

Shortly after that, Periphas' scouts had found Hylas and Pirra and helped them down the mountain. Hylas had refused to be taken to the main camp; he'd insisted they pitch their own small camp above it in the hills—because of Havoc, and Issi, who wouldn't go near warriors, whether they were rebel or Crow.

That had been three days ago—and still Hylas couldn't see. This morning, a boy had arrived from the main camp, bringing Jinx, and a summons to the High Chieftain's tent.

Hylas rode, with Pirra on foot, holding Jinx's bridle. Hylas *hated* that, he hated being helpless and blind. Last night, he'd overheard Pirra asking Hekabi if the Lady of Fire had taken his sight in return for sparing his life. He'd wondered that too, but the fact that Pirra hadn't mentioned it to his face made it even worse.

"I can still ride, you know," he told her between his teeth.

"I know, but you can't see what's coming—"

"There's no need to treat me like a child!"

"Fine," she snapped. "Next time I see you heading for a low branch, I'll just let it knock you off, shall I?"

He didn't reply. After Hekabi's eye-baths and Havoc's assiduous licking, he could just about distinguish night from day, but faces remained a total blur.

"You've got to be patient," said Pirra.

"You try it," he flung back.

These days, they bickered constantly; it helped keep the fear at bay. Not even Hekabi knew if he would ever see clearly again.

And then what? he thought as Jinx picked his way down the hill. If I can't see, I can't hunt. I'll be no use to anyone . . .

He told himself he had much to be thankful for. They'd all survived, and thanks to Hekabi, Akastos was recovering from his wounds. But somehow, Hylas couldn't *feel* it. He was jumpy and irritable. He couldn't talk to Pirra, couldn't tell her he had nightmares every night, flashes from the battle and Telamon screaming as the lightning struck . . .

Even finding Issi again wasn't the joyous reunion he'd longed for, because he couldn't *see* her—and she couldn't speak. "It happens sometimes," Hekabi had said. "It might be years before she speaks—if she ever does." Hylas had tried to talk to his sister, but it was hopeless when he couldn't see her face. She spent much of her time in the hills with Havoc, and seemed ill at ease with Pirra.

"Maybe she thinks I'm in the way," Pirra suggested. "That I've sort of—taken her place?"

But Issi was his *sister;* how could that be?

They'd reached Akastos' tent. Hylas asked Pirra if she was coming in too, but she was still cross with him, and stomped off to water Jinx.

Inside, he made out the blurred figures of what he guessed was Akastos, reclining on a cot, with Hekabi kneeling beside him. To Hylas' astonishment, they were laughing so hard that Hekabi was rocking back and forth and Akastos was clutching his bandaged side.

They welcomed Hylas, but he sensed the current between them and felt out of place. "I'll come back later," he said curtly.

"No, Flea, you'll stay," said Akastos with a smile in his voice.

Hylas heard Hekabi rise to her feet. "Don't talk too long," she told Akastos softly. "You need to rest." As she passed Hylas, he felt her cool hand at his temple. "Your visions," she said. "They've gone."

He nodded. "I realized when I couldn't sense Telamon's ghost. I think maybe the lightning blasted them away."

"Maybe." She too had a smile in her voice. "And lions are sacred to the Lady of Fire: Perhaps Havoc licked them away."

When she was gone, Hylas groped toward Akastos' cot and sat cross-legged beside it. He felt awkward; it was the first time they'd been together since the battle. "How do you feel?" he asked.

"Sore," Akastos said drily. "You?"

"The same."

Then Akastos asked what Hylas had been dreading: He wanted to know what had happened on the battlefield after he'd passed out. Haltingly, Hylas told him, about the Angry Ones dropping from the sky, and the ghost of Akastos' brother licking the blood of vengeance from its lips.

"What did he look like?" said Akastos with a catch in his voice.

"Like you, but younger. And he—he was missing his little finger."

"Ah. So it really was him." He was silent for a while. "Strange," he murmured. "When you've wanted something for years and you finally get it, it's hard to take in."

"I know," said Hylas with feeling. He was thinking of Issi.

"It's a long way from the Island of the Fin People, isn't it, Flea? When I talked you down from that woodpile."

"You didn't—you *tricked* me down."

Akastos chuckled. "So I did!"

Belatedly, Hylas realized that he was speaking with the High Chieftain of Mycenae. "What will you do now?" he asked.

"Rebuild. Restore order to Akea. Do my best to heal the wounds of the past."

From what Hylas had heard, he'd already started. The rains had quenched the fire at Lapithos before the main grain stores were destroyed, and Akastos had ordered food to be distributed to the peasants. He'd also earned the respect of the surviving Crows by forbidding reprisals against them, and decreeing honorable rites for their dead. Telamon's body had been burned, and at Hylas' request, the ashes had been placed beside his father in the tomb of his Ancestors. The ashes of Koronos and Pharax had been given no rites, and merely scattered on the wind.

As for the dagger, Hekabi had gathered all the fragments she could find, and cast them into rivers and streams, to be washed down to the Sea and lost forever.

"There's a lot to do," Akastos said quietly. "Soon, I'll return to Mycenae. Periphas will stay here and rule Lykonia."

"That's good," said Hylas. "He'll make a fine leader."

Akastos paused. "So will you. I want you to take Messenia."

"What?"

"The chieftaincy. You saved my life on the battlefield, Hylas, I don't forget. And I want a chieftain I can trust."

"You can't have a blind chieftain," growled Hylas.

"I meant, if you get your sight back."

Hylas scowled. "Not even then," he said harshly. "If I ruled, I'd have to fight. That's what rulers do."

"Sometimes."

"How can you bear it?" Hylas burst out. "Every night

I'm back in the battle! I've just killed a man, I can feel the drag on my sword as I pull it out of his flesh . . . And I see Telamon . . ." His voice cracked. "He used to be my *friend,* and I tricked him into getting struck by lightning!"

"That's war, Hylas," Akastos said in a hard voice.

"Well, I want no part of it!"

"No one does! But sometimes you have to fight to defend what's yours!"

Hylas glowered. He felt the High Chieftain's strong hand on his shoulder. "I know how it is," said Akastos. "You can't get the bad things out of your mind, and they're cutting you off from Pirra and your sister. But they'll *fade,* Hylas. I promise." Then he said in a brisker tone: "So tell me, what can I do for you? There must be something you want."

Hylas thought. "Um—yes. Actually, two things."

Akastos laughed and cuffed him around the head. "Ah, Flea! You haven't changed that much after all!"

Echo swooped past Pirra, then plunged into a flock of rock-doves, scattering them for fun. Pirra laughed. Hylas didn't notice. He was limping beside her, scowling at the ground.

It was four days since he'd had his talk with Akastos. His sight was nearly restored: Yesterday, he'd even downed a squirrel with his slingshot; but he remained unhappy and withdrawn.

Pirra wanted the old Hylas back. She wanted . . . She

kept thinking about that moment before he'd left her on the trail to ride after Telamon, when she'd kissed him and he'd kissed her back. She would quite like to do it again.

I suppose it'll be down to me as usual, she thought as they climbed the hill toward camp. I'll just have to *say* something.

She was mustering her courage to begin when Issi appeared between the trees with Havoc, and the moment was lost.

"Issi!" called Hylas. But Issi had spotted Pirra. She hesitated, as if trying to pluck up the courage to join them. Then she melted back into the forest.

"What's the *matter* with her?" exclaimed Hylas.

"I told you," said Pirra in exasperation, "she still feels left out. She'll come around in time."

"But *why* would she feel left out?"

She flung up her arms. "Well, because all the time she was hiding out in Messenia, we were together!" She reddened. "I mean, not *together* exactly, but—"

"But I'm her *brother*! What does she think, that I'll abandon her?"

"Of course not! It's just—a lot for her to get used to. I mean, me being, um, with you. Maybe you need to reassure her."

"How?"

Pirra looked at him. She heaved a sigh. Until things were sorted out between him and Issi, there was no *point* talking to him about anything else; he wouldn't take it in.

When they reached their camp, she threw down her waterskin and put her hands on her hips. "I've had an idea. I think it might help you with Issi."

"What is it?" he said.

She told him. And for the first time since the battle, he broke into a grin.

"I told you, it's a surprise," said Hylas for the tenth time as they were making their way through the marshes.

Issi drew a frog in the mud, then made a huge arc with her arms.

He laughed. "No, it's not a giant frog."

Issi scowled and kicked him in the shin. *Tell me!*

"No!" He made a grab at her, but she dodged and went splashing ahead with Havoc. Hylas felt a pang of love and apprehension. This had better work.

Over his shoulder, he gave Pirra a rueful smile. She'd offered to stay behind in Lykonia so that he could be alone with Issi, but he'd said no, Issi had to get used to her. Pirra had flushed with pleasure. He'd wanted to take her in his arms and kiss her; but he had to make things right with Issi first.

The Marsh Dwellers had greeted them with respectful bows and a basket of fish for Havoc, and their pudgy faces had lit up when they'd seen Issi. Hylas had asked if they'd really never suspected that the Outsider "boy" they'd sheltered might be a girl, but they'd shaken their heads. "Why would we?" they'd said with startling simplicity.

"She wore the brown headband, so we took her for a boy."

By the time they reached the Sea, Issi was bursting with impatience. This had better work, thought Hylas again.

Havoc bounded into the shallows. Hylas lifted Issi and flung her in. She surfaced, spluttering with laughter, and he dived in after her. Pirra sat on a rock and watched.

Hylas came up shaking the water from his hair. "Time to show you why I brought you," he told Issi. "It's something incredibly special that I know you'll love."

Treading water, she splashed him impatiently.

"Just *wait!*" He gave a piercing whistle and smacked the waves with the flat of his hand. They waited. *Please, please come,* prayed Hylas. *Help me as you've helped so often before.*

Havoc shot out of the shallows and stood on the shore, staring seaward. A moment later, out in the bay, something flashed.

Issi gasped. Hylas began to smile.

Spirit leaped clear of the Sea in a great shining arc, then smacked down in a shower of spray and sped toward them. On her rock, Pirra put her fist to her forehead and bowed. Spirit was her friend, but he was also a creature sacred to the Goddess.

The dolphin brushed against Hylas, who stroked his flank. *Thank you, Spirit,* he told his friend silently. Issi was looking on round-eyed.

"Don't touch his blow-hole," Hylas warned. "And be careful not to scratch." He was about to go on, but Spirit slid past Issi upside down, and she trailed her fingers lightly over his belly. Hylas moved back to give them space. The dolphin swam past Issi again, the right way up—and without being told, she took hold of his fin with both hands and he was off, pulling her after him while she lay at full stretch, flying over the waves and grinning from ear to ear.

She spent all afternoon playing with Spirit, and in the end, Hylas had to haul her bodily out of the Sea. As they started on the return journey, Havoc—who'd gone off when the dolphin had appeared—came and rubbed against Hylas, as if to claim him, now that he was back on land.

Pirra walked some distance behind, so that he and Issi could be alone. "Issi," he began awkwardly. "You know that I never stopped trying to find you. You do know that, don't you?"

Issi nodded, but she kept her eyes on the ground.

"And you mustn't *ever* think that because Pirra is with me, you'll be—left out. That's just not how it is. You're my sister." He cleared his throat. "You're—part of me."

Scowling, Issi chewed a reed stem. She was as embarrassed as he. "And whenever you want," he went on hurriedly, "we can come down to the Sea and visit Spirit, just you and me. Yes?"

Issi thought about that. Then she clawed the air with both hands, made a snarly face, and gave a silent roar.

Hylas blinked. Then he broke into a grin. "Of course Havoc can come too!"

Issi nodded. She turned and gave Pirra a small, tentative smile over her shoulder: *And you can come as well.* Then she put her hand in Hylas' and grinned up at him. And for the first time since he'd first caught sight of her on the Ancestor Peak, he truly felt that he had found his sister again.

They'd been back in their little camp for a day, and Hylas knew he couldn't put it off any longer. Issi was snuggled against Havoc, fast asleep; so he could be alone with Pirra.

He found her by the stream a short distance from camp, combing her hair. She threw him a wary look, but didn't speak.

You've got to ask her *now*, he told himself fiercely. Just say, will you be my girl?

But he was so nervous that instead he blurted out: "This morning I made an offering to the Lady of the Wild Things."

She blinked. "What did you ask for?"

"Um—it was for Telamon."

"*Telamon?* He would have killed you!"

"I know, but . . . He was my friend once. I want his spirit to be at peace."

"And that's what matters to you, is it?" she said crossly. "Someone who used to be a friend, and became a deadly enemy?"

"No, I mean . . . Look, I didn't come to talk about Telamon."

"Glad to hear it!" Her cheeks were flushed, her hair a black cloud around her shoulders. She caught him looking at her, and her flush deepened.

There was an awkward silence. Just *ask* her, Hylas told himself.

The silence lengthened. Pirra blew out a long breath and rose to her feet. Without so much as a glance at him, she tied back her hair with a twist of grass and stalked toward camp.

Grinding his teeth, Hylas started after her. That was when the gods gave him another chance. He spotted a boy coming toward him, bringing a gift from the High Chieftain: Jinx and a beautiful gray mare.

"Ah, that's good!" cried Hylas. Then to Pirra: "Pirra, come back!"

"Why? What for?"

"You take the mare, I'll take Jinx! Come on, we're going for a walk!"

"Where?"

"I'll tell you when we get there, it's not far!"

The light was turning golden and the shadows were lengthening as they led the horses uphill toward a meadow dotted with olive trees.

Hylas' elation drained away, and with every step, his nervousness grew. "I didn't tell you before," he said to Pirra, "but Akastos offered me the chieftaincy of Messenia. I—I turned it down."

To his surprise, she nodded. "Yes, I told him you would."

"How did you know?"

"Well—I know you."

He shot her a glance. "And you don't—mind?"

"No, why should I?"

"I—we—would have been rich."

"I've been rich. It didn't make me happy."

They walked on a bit farther. Then he said, "Akastos asked me what I wanted, and I said, two things."

"Oh?"

"First, I said I wanted to set Jinx free, with a mare to keep him company."

Pirra pressed her lips together and nodded. "That's good. He ought to have a mate."

He shot her another glance. "Yes, I think so too. It's good to—to have a mate."

"Yes," she replied evenly.

They reached the meadow, and Hylas slipped off the mare's bridle. She trotted a few steps, then put down her head and grazed.

Hylas stroked Jinx's bony nose for the last time. "Goodbye, Jinx," he said softly. "Enjoy your freedom." He took off the bridle. Jinx nuzzled his neck, then ambled toward the mare, who'd stopped grazing and was watching him intently. They touched noses. The mare cantered off across the meadow. Jinx flicked up his tail and cantered after her.

"What was the second thing you asked for?" said Pirra, keeping her eyes on the horses.

"I asked him to give me somewhere in the mountains, where there are no peasants and no warriors, so that—so that Havoc can come too. And Issi."

Pirra nodded. Her color was high. He could see a pulse beating in her throat.

Havoc appeared out of nowhere and rubbed against his thigh. She cast an indifferent eye on the horses, having recently made a kill, then ambled over to Issi, who'd come to see what was happening. Clearly sensing that she shouldn't butt in, Issi climbed an olive tree, where she sat, swinging her legs, discreetly looking the other way.

Echo swept past, her wing beats lifting tendrils of Pirra's black hair, then soared skyward with a joyful shriek.

Hylas took a deep breath. "Will you come and live with me in the mountains?" he said to Pirra in a rush. "I mean—as my girl?"

At last, she turned and looked up at him. Her dark eyes were shining, her lips curved in the beginnings of a smile.

He was about to pull her into his arms, but Havoc nosed between them, nearly knocking them over. In her tree, Issi clamped her hands over her mouth to muffle her giggles.

"Oh, Havoc!" muttered Hylas, pushing the lioness out of the way.

Pirra gave a little spurt of laughter. "Of course I will," she said.

Author's Note

*W*arrior Bronze* takes place three and a half thousand years ago during the Bronze Age, in what we call ancient Greece. We don't know much about Bronze Age Greece, as its people left so few written records, but we do know something about their astonishing cultures, which we call the Mycenaeans and the Minoans. (Hylas is Mycenaean, and Pirra is Minoan.)

It's thought that this was a world of scattered chieftaincies, separated by mountain ranges and forests, and that it was wetter and greener than today, with far more wild animals both on land and sea. Also, this was long before the Ancient Greeks ranged their gods into an orderly pantheon of Zeus, Hera, Hades, and so on. That's why the gods Hylas and Pirra worship have different names: They were the forerunners of the later lot.

To create the world of Hylas and Pirra, I've studied the archaeology of the Greek Bronze Age. To get an idea of people's beliefs, I've drawn on those of more recent peoples who still live in traditional ways, as I did in my Stone Age series, Chronicles of Ancient Darkness. And although most people in Hylas' time lived by farming or fishing, I think much of the knowledge and beliefs of the Stone Age hunter-gatherers would have survived into the Bronze Age, particularly among poorer people, such as Hylas himself.

Concerning place names, Akea (or Achaea, as it's often spelled) is the ancient name for mainland Greece, and Lykonia is my name for the region which today is called Lakonia. I haven't changed the name Mycenae, as it's so well known. And I've used the name Keftian for the great Cretan civilization we call Minoan. (We don't know what they called themselves; depending on which book you read, their name may have been Keftians, or that may have been a name given them by the ancient Egyptians.)

The map of the World of Gods and Warriors shows the world as Hylas and Pirra experience it, so it leaves out many places and islands that don't come into the story, and includes others that I made up, such as the Island of the Fin People and Thalakrea. The same goes for the map of Akea; this features only those places that are relevant to the story in *Warrior Bronze*.

Warrior Bronze brings Hylas back to the mountains where his adventures began, so I've drawn extensively on the research trips to Greece that I made for the earlier books in the series. In particular, I've drawn on the time I spent in Lakonia, especially: the Langada Gorge that winds through the Taÿgetos Mountains; the area around the top of the Langada Pass, which I explored for several days; and the coast and caves at Vlychada, on the Bay of Diros in southwest Lakonia.

I will always be grateful to Todd Whitelaw, Professor of Aegean Archaeology at the Institute of Archaeology, University College London, for patiently reading and commenting on each manuscript, and providing me with many helpful pointers on various aspects of Bronze Age life. I also want to thank my editor at Puffin Books, Ben Horslen, for his lively and imaginative response to the story of Hylas and Pirra. Finally, as always, my thanks to my wonderful and immensely talented agent Peter Cox, for his never-failing commitment and support.

Michelle Paver, 2015

INTERNATIONAL BESTSELLING AUTHOR

MICHELLE PAVER

is an avid researcher who tirelessly investigates the worlds she creates—traveling extensively in the wild, encountering bears, boars, and wolves, and swimming with dolphins and killer whales. Her bestselling novels bring the past vividly and excitingly to life, including the critically acclaimed *Wolf Brother*, the first book in her award-winning Chronicles of Ancient Darkness series.

www.michellepaver.com